More Oddments

Other Five Star Titles by Bill Pronzini:

All the Long Years: Western Stories
Oddments: A Short Story Collection
Sleuths

More Oddments

Bill Pronzini

Five Star • Waterville, Maine

Five Star First Edition Mystery Series.

Published in 2001 in conjunction with
Tekno Books and Ed Gorman.

Set in 11 pt. Plantin by Al Chase.

Printed in the United States on permanent paper.

Library of Congress Cataloging-in-Publication Data

Pronzini, Bill.
More oddments : a short story collection / Bill Pronzini.
p. cm.—(Five Star first edition mystery series)
ISBN 0-7862-3557-8 (hc : alk. paper)
1. Detective and mystery stories, American. I. Title.
II. Series.
PS3566.R67 M67 2001

2001050162

Contents

Fergus O'Hara,

Detective

On a balmy March afternoon in the third full year of the War Between the States, while that conflict continued to rage bloodily some two thousand miles distant, Fergus and Hattie O'Hara jostled their way along San Francisco's Embarcadero toward Long Wharf and the riverboat *Delta Star*. The half-plank, half-dirt roads and plank walks were choked with horses, mules, cargo-laden wagons—and with all manner of humanity: bearded miners and burly roustabouts and sun-darkened farmers; rope-muscled Kanakas and Filipino laborers and coolie-hatted Chinese; shrewd-eyed merchants and ruffle-shirted gamblers and bonneted ladies who might have been the wives of prominent citizens or trollops on their way to the gold fields of the Mother Lode. Both the pace and the din were furious. At exactly four P.M. some twenty steamers would leave the waterfront, bound upriver for Sacramento and Stockton and points in between.

O'Hara clung to their carpetbags and Hattie clung to O'Hara as they pushed through the throng. They could see the *Delta Star* the moment they reached Long Wharf. She was an impressive side-wheeler, one of the "floating palaces" that had adorned the Sacramento and San Joaquin rivers for more than ten years. Powered by a single-cylinder, vertical-beam engine, she was 245 feet long and had slim, graceful lines. The long rows of windows running full length both starboard and larboard along her deckhouse, where the Gentlemen's and Dining Saloons and most of the staterooms were located, refracted jewel-like the rays of the afternoon sun. Above, to the stern, was the weather deck, on which stretched the "texas"; this housed luxury staterooms and cabins for the packet's officers. Some distance forward of the texas was the oblong glassed-in structure of the pilothouse.

Smiling as they approached, O'Hara said, "Now ain't she a fine lady?" He spoke with a careless brogue, the result of a strict ethnic upbringing in the Irish Channel section of New Orleans. At times this caused certain individuals to underestimate his capabilities and intelligence, which in his profession was a major asset.

"She *is* fine, Fergus," Hattie agreed. "As fine as any on the Mississippi before the war. How far did you say it was to Stockton?"

O'Hara laughed. "A hundred twenty-seven miles. One night in the lap of luxury is all we'll be having this trip, me lady."

"Pity," Hattie said. She was in her late twenties, five years younger than her husband; dark-complected, buxom. Thick black hair, worn in ringlets, was covered by a lace-decorated bonnet. She wore a gray serge traveling dress, the hem of which was now coated with dust.

O'Hara was tall and plump, and sported a luxuriant red beard of which he was inordinately proud and on which he doted every morning with scissors and comb. Like Hattie, he had mild blue eyes; unlike Hattie, and as a result of a fondness for spirits, he possessed a nose that approximated the color of his beard. He was dressed in a black frock coat, striped trousers, and a flowered vest. He carried no visible weapons but in a holster inside his coat was a double-action revolver.

The *Delta Star*'s stageplank, set aft to the main deck, was jammed with passengers and wagons; it was now twenty till four. A large group of nankeen-dressed men were congregated near the foot of the plank. All of them wore green felt shamrocks pinned to the lapels of their coats, and several were smoking thin, "long-nine" seegars. Fluttering above them on a pole held by one was a green banner with the words *Mulrooney Guards, San Francisco Company A* crudely printed on it in white.

Four of the group were struggling to lift a massive wooden crate that appeared to be quite heavy. They managed to get it aloft, grunting, and began to stagger with it to the plank. As they started up, two members of the *Delta Star*'s deck crew came down and blocked their way. One of them said, "Before you go any farther, gents, show us your manifest on that box."

One of the other Mulrooneys stepped up the plank. "What manifest?" he demanded. "This ain't cargo, it's personal belongings."

"Anything heavy as that pays cargo," the deckhand said.

"Rules is rules and they apply to Bluebellies same as to better folks."

"Bluebellies, is it? Ye damned Copperhead, I'll pound ye up into horsemeat!" And the Mulrooney hit the deckhand on the side of the head and knocked him down.

The second crew member stepped forward and hit the Mulrooney on the side of the head and knocked *him* down.

Another of the Guards jumped in and hit the second crewman on the side of the head and knocked *him* down.

The first deckhand got up and the first Mulrooney got up, minus his hat, and began swinging at each other. The second crewman got up and began swinging at the second Mulrooney. The other members of the Guards, shouting encouragement, formed a tight circle around the fighting men—all except for the four carrying the heavy wooden crate. Those Mulrooneys struggled up the stageplank with their burden and disappeared among the confusion on the main deck.

The fight did not last long. Several roustabouts and one of the steamer's mates hurried onto the landing and broke it up. No one seemed to have been injured, save for the two deck-hands who were both unconscious. The mate seemed undecided as to what to do, finally concluded that to do nothing at all was the best recourse; he turned up the plank again. Four roustabouts carried the limp crewmen up after him, followed by the Guards who were all now loudly singing "John Brown's Body."

Hattie asked O'Hara, "Now what was *that* all about?"

"War business," he told her solemnly. "California's a long way from the battlefields, but feelings and loyalties are as strong here as in the East."

"But who are the Mulrooney Guards?"

Before O'Hara could answer, a tall man wearing a Prince Albert, who was standing next to Hattie, swung toward them and smiled and said, "I couldn't help overhearing the lady's question. If you'll pardon the intrusion, I can supply an answer."

O'Hara looked the tall man over and decided he was a gambler. He had no particular liking for gamblers, but for the most part he was tolerant of them. He said the intrusion was pardoned, introduced himself and Hattie, and learned that the tall man was John A. Colfax, of San Francisco.

Colfax had gray eyes that were both congenial and cunning. In his left hand he continually shuffled half a dozen small bronze war-issue cents—coinage that was not often seen in the West. He said, "The Mulrooney Guards is a more or less official militia company, one of several supporting the Union cause. They have two companies, one in San Francisco and one in Stockton. I imagine this one is joining the other for some sort of celebration."

"Tomorrow is St. Patrick's Day," O'Hara told him.

"Ah, yes, of course."

"Ye seem to know quite a bit about these lads, Mr. Colfax."

"I am a regular passenger on the *Delta Star*," Colfax said. "On the Sacramento packets as well. A traveling man picks up a good deal of information."

O'Hara said blandly, "Aye, that he does."

Hattie said, "I wonder what the Mulrooneys have in that crate?"

Colfax allowed as how he had no idea. He seemed about to say something further, but the appearance of three closely grouped men, hurrying through the crowd toward the stageplank, claimed his attention. The one in the middle, O'Hara saw, wore a broadcloth suit and a nervous, harried expression; cradled in both hands against his body was a large and apparently heavy valise. The two men on either side were more roughly dressed, had revolvers holstered at their hips. Their expressions were dispassionate, their eyes watchful.

O'Hara frowned and glanced at Colfax. The gambler watched the trio climb the plank and hurry up the aft stairway; then he said quietly, as if to himself, "It appears we'll be carrying more than passengers and cargo this trip." He regarded the O'Haras again, touched his hat, said it had been a pleasure talking to them, and moved away to board the riverboat.

Hattie looked at her husband inquiringly. He said, "Gold."

"Gold, Fergus?"

"That nervous chap had the look of a banker, the other two of deputies. A bank transfer of specie or dust from here to Stockton—or so I'm thinking."

"Where will they keep it?"

"Purser's office, mayhap. Or the pilothouse."

Hattie and O'Hara climbed the plank. As they were crossing the main deck, the three men appeared again on the stairway; the one in the broadcloth suit looked considerably less nervous now. O'Hara watched them go down onto the landing. Then, shrugging, he followed Hattie up the stairs to the weather deck. They stopped at the starboard rail to await departure.

Hattie said, "What did you think of Mr. Colfax?"

"A slick-tongued lad, even for a gambler. But ye'd not want to be giving him a coin to put in a village poor box for ye."

She laughed. "He seemed rather interested in the delivery of gold, if that's what it was."

"Aye, so he did."

At exactly four o'clock the *Delta Star*'s whistle sounded; her buckets churned the water, steam poured from her twin stacks. She began to move slowly away from the wharf. All up and down the Embarcadero now, whistles sounded and the other packets commenced backing down from their landings. The waters of the bay took on a chaotic appearance as the boats maneuvered for right-of-way. Clouds of steam filled the sky; the sound of pilot whistles was angry and shrill.

Once the *Delta Star* was clear of the wharves and of other riverboats, her speed increased steadily. Hattie and O'Hara remained at the rail until San Francisco's low, sun-washed skyline had receded into the distance; then they went in search of a steward, who took them to their stateroom. Its windows faced larboard, but its entrance was located inside a tunnel-like hallway down the center of the texas. Spacious and opulent, the cabin contained carved rosewood paneling and red plush upholstery. Hattie said she thought it was grand. O'Hara, who had never been particularly impressed by Victorian elegance, said he imagined she would be wanting to freshen up a bit—and that, so as not to be disturbing her, he would take a stroll about the decks.

"Stay away from the liquor buffet," Hattie said. "The day is young, if I make my meaning clear."

O'Hara sighed. "I had no intention of visiting the liquor buffet," he lied, and sighed again, and left the stateroom.

He wandered aft, past the officers' quarters. When he emerged from the texas he found himself confronted by the huge A-shaped gallows frame that housed the cylinder, valve gear, beam and crank of the walking-beam engine. Each stroke of the piston produced a mighty roar and hiss of escaping steam. The noise turned O'Hara around and sent him back through the texas to the forward stairway.

Ahead of him as he started down were two men who had come out of the pilothouse. One was tall, with bushy black hair and a thick mustache—apparently a passenger. The second wore a square-billed cap and the sort of stern, authoritative look that would have identified him as the *Delta Star*'s pilot even without the cap. At this untroubled point in the journey, the packet would be in the hands of a cub apprentice.

The door to the Gentlemen's Saloon kept intruding on O'Hara's thoughts as he walked about the deckhouse. Finally he went down to the main deck. Here, in the open areas and in the shed-like expanse beneath the superstructures, deck passengers and cargo were pressed together in noisy confusion: men and women and children, wagons and animals and chickens in coops; sacks, bales, boxes, hogsheads, cords of bull pine for the roaring fireboxes under the boilers. And, too, the Mulrooney Guards, who were loosely grouped near the taffrail, alternately singing "The Girl I Left Behind Me" and passing around jugs of what was likely poteen—a powerful homemade Irish whiskey.

O'Hara sauntered near the group, stood with his back against a stanchion, and began to shave cuttings from his tobacco plug into his briar. One of the Mulrooneys—small and fair and feisty looking—noticed him, studied his luxuriant red beard, and then approached him carrying one of the jugs. Without preamble he demanded to know if the gentleman were Irish. O'Hara said he was, with great dignity. The Mulrooney slapped him on the back. "I knew it!" he said effusively. "Me name's Billy Culligan. Have a drap of the crayture."

O'Hara decided Hattie had told him only to stay away from the buffet. There was no deceit in accepting hospitality from fellows of the Auld Sod. He took the jug, drank deeply, and allowed as how it was a fine crayture, indeed. Then he introduced himself, saying that he and the missus were traveling to Stockton on a business matter.

"Ye won't be conducting business on the morrow, will ye?"

"On St. Pat's Day?" O'Hara was properly shocked.

"Boyo, I like ye," Culligan said. "How would ye like to join in on the biggest St. Pat's Day celebration in the entire sovereign state of California?"

"I'd like nothing better."

"Then come to Green Park, on the north of Stockton, 'twixt nine and ten and tell the lads ye're a friend of Billy Culligan. There'll be a parade, and all the food and liquor ye can hold. Oh, it'll be a fine celebration, lad!"

O'Hara said he and the missus would be there, meaning it. Culligan offered another drink of poteen, which O'Hara casually accepted. Then the little Mulrooney stepped forward and said in a conspiratorial voice, "Come round here to the taffrail just before we steam into Stockton on the morrow. We've a plan to start off St. Pat's Day with a mighty salute—part of the reason we sent our wives and wee ones ahead on the *San Joaquin*. Ye won't want to be missing that either." Before O'Hara could ask him what he meant by "mighty salute," he and his jug were gone into the midst of the other Guards.

"Me lady," O'Hara said contentedly, "that was a meal fit for royalty and no doubt about it."

Hattie agreed that it had been a sumptuous repast as they walked from the Dining Saloon to the texas stairway. The evening was mild, with little breeze and no sign of the thick tule fog that often made Northern California riverboating a hazardous proposition. The *Delta Star*—aglow with hundreds of lights—had come through the Carquinez Straits, passed Chipp's Island, and was now entering the San Joaquin River. A pale moon silvered the water, turned a ghostly white the long stretches of fields along both banks.

On the weather deck, they stood close together at the larboard rail, not far from the pilothouse. For a couple of minutes they were alone. Then footsteps sounded and O'Hara turned to see the ship's captain and pilot returning from their dinner. Touching his cap, the captain—a lean, graying man of fifty-odd—wished them good evening. The pilot merely grunted.

The O'Haras continued to stand looking out at the willows and cottonwoods along the riverbank. Then, suddenly, an explosive, angry cry came from the pilothouse, startling them both. This was followed by muffled voices, another sharp exclamation, movement not clearly perceived through the window glass and beyond partially drawn rear curtains, and several sharp blasts on the pilot whistle.

Natural curiosity drew O'Hara away from the rail, hurrying; Hattie was close behind him. The door to the pilothouse stood open when they reached it, and O'Hara turned inside by one step. The enclosure was almost as opulent as their stateroom, but he noticed its appointments only peripherally. What captured his full attention was three men now grouped before the wheel, and the four items on the floor close to and against the starboard bulkhead.

The pilot stood clutching two of the wheel spokes, red-faced with anger; the captain was bending over the kneeling figure of the third man—a young blond individual wearing a buttoned-up sack coat and baggy trousers, both of which were streaked with dust and soot and grease. The blond lad was making soft moaning sounds, holding the back of his head cupped in one palm.

One of the items on the floor was a steel pry bar. The others were a small safe bolted to the bulkhead, a black valise—the one O'Hara had seen carried by the nervous man and his two bodyguards—and a medium-sized iron strongbox, just large enough to have fit inside the valise. The safe door, minus its combination dial, stood wide open; the valise and a strongbox were also open. All three were quite obviously empty.

The pilot jerked the bell knobs, signaling an urgent request to the engineer for a lessening of speed, and began barking stand-by orders into a speaking tube. His was the voice which had startled Hattie and O'Hara. The captain was saying to the blond man, "It's a miracle we didn't drift out of the channel and run afoul of a snag—a miracle, Chadwick."

"I can't be held to blame, sir," Chadwick said defensively. "Whoever it was hit me from behind. I was sitting at the wheel when I heard the door open and thought it was you and Mr. Bridgeman returning from supper, so I didn't even bother to turn. The next thing, my head seemed to explode. That is all I know."

He managed to regain his feet and moved stiffly to a red plush sofa, hitching up his trousers with one hand; the other still held the back of his head. Bridgeman, the pilot, banged down the speaking tube, then spun the wheel a half-turn to larboard. As he did the last, he glanced over his shoulder and saw O'Hara and Hattie. "Get out of here!" he shouted at them. "There is nothing here for you."

"Perhaps, now, that isn't true," O'Hara said mildly. "Ye've had a robbery, have ye not?"

"That is none of your affair."

Boldly O'Hara came deeper into the pilothouse, motioning Hattie to close the door. She did so. Bridgeman yelled, "I told you to get out of here! Who do you think you are?"

"Fergus O'Hara—operative of the Pinkerton Police Agency."

Bridgeman stared at him, open-mouthed. The captain and Chadwick had shifted their attention to him as well. At length, in a less harsh tone, the pilot said, "Pinkerton Agency?"

"Of Chicago, Illinois; Allan Pinkerton, Principal."

O'Hara produced his billfold, extracted from it the letter from Allan Pinkerton and the Chicago & Eastern Central Railroad Pass, both of which identified him, as the bearer of these documents, to be a Pinkerton Police agent. He showed them to both Bridgeman and the captain.

"What would a Pinkerton man be doing way out here in California?" the captain asked.

"Me wife Hattie and me are on the trail of a gang that has been terrorizing Adams Express coaches. We've traced them to San Francisco and now have reliable information they're to be found in Stockton."

"Your *wife* is a Pinkerton agent too? A *woman . . . ?*"

O'Hara looked at him as if he might be a dullard. "Ye've never heard of Miss Kate Warne, one of the agency's most trusted Chicago operatives? No, I don't suppose ye have. Well, me wife has no official capacity, but since one of the leaders of this gang is reputed to be a woman, and since Hattie has assisted me in the past, women being able to obtain information in places men cannot, I've brought her along."

Bridgeman said from the wheel, "Well, we can use a trained detective after what has happened here."

O'Hara nodded. "Is it gold ye've had stolen?"

"Gold—yes. How did you know that?"

He told them of witnessing the delivery of the valise at Long Wharf. He asked then, "How large an amount is involved?"

"Forty thousand dollars," the captain said.

O'Hara whistled. "That's a fair considerable sum."

"To put it mildly, sir."

"Was it specie or dust?"

"Dust. An urgent consignment from the California Merchant's Bank to their branch in Stockton."

"How many men had foreknowledge of the shipment?"

"The officials of the bank, Mr. Bridgeman, and myself."

"No other officers of the packet?"

"No."

"Would you be telling me, Captain, who was present when the delivery was made this afternoon?"

"Mr. Bridgeman and I, and a friend of his visiting in San Francisco—a newspaperman from Nevada."

O'Hara remembered the tall man with bushy hair who had been with the pilot earlier. "Can ye vouch for this newspaperman?" he asked Bridgeman.

"I can. His reputation is unimpeachable."

"Has anyone other than he been here since the gold was brought aboard?"

"Not to my knowledge."

Chadwick said that no one had come by while he was on duty, and none of them had noticed anyone shirking about at any time. The captain said sourly, "It appears as though almost any man on this packet could be the culprit. Just how do you propose we find out which one, Mr. O'Hara?"

O'Hara did not reply. He bent to examine the safe. The combination dial appeared to have been snapped off, by a hand with experience at such villainous business. The valise and the strong-box had also been forced. The pry bar was an ordinary tool and had likely also been used as a weapon to knock Chadwick unconscious.

He straightened and moved about the enclosure, studying each fixture. Then he got down on hands and knees and peered under both the sofa and a blackened winter stove. It was under the stove that he found the coin.

His fingers grasped it, closed it into his palm. Standing again, he glanced at the coin and saw that it was made of bronze, a small war-issue cent piece shinily new and free of dust or soot. A smile plucked at the edges of his mouth as he slipped the coin into his vest pocket.

Bridgeman said, "Did you find something?"

"Perhaps. Then again, perhaps not."

O'Hara came forward, paused near where Bridgeman stood at the wheel. Through the windshield he could see the moonlit waters of the San Joaquin. He could also see, as a result of the pilothouse lamps and the darkness without, his own dim reflection in the glass. He thought his stern expression was rather like the one Allan Pinkerton himself possessed.

Bridgeman suggested that crewmen be posted on the lower decks throughout the night, as a precaution in the event the culprit had a confederate with a boat somewhere along the route and intended to leave the packet in the wee hours. The captain thought this was a good idea; so did O'Hara.

He was ready to leave, but the captain had a few more words for him. "I am grateful for your professional assistance, Mr. O'Hara, but as master of the *Delta Star* the primary investigative responsibility is mine. Please inform me immediately if you learn anything of significance."

O'Hara said he would.

"Also, I intend my inquiries to be discreet, so as not to alarm the passengers. I'll expect yours to be the same."

"Discretion is me middle name," O'Hara assured him.

A few moments later, he and Hattie were on their way back along the larboard rail to the texas. Hattie, who had been silent during their time in the pilothouse, started to speak, but O'Hara overrode her. "I know what ye're going to say, me lady, and it'll do no good. Me mind's made up. The opportunity to sniff out forty thousand in missing gold is one I'll not pass up."

He left Hattie at the door to their stateroom and hurried to the deckhouse, where he entered the Gentlemen's Saloon. It was a long room, with a liquor buffet at one end and private tables and card layouts spread throughout. A pall of tobacco smoke as thick as tule fog hung in the crowded enclosure.

O'Hara located the shrewd, handsome features of John A. Colfax at a table aft. Two other men were with him: a portly individual with sideburns like miniature tumbleweeds, and the mustached Nevada reporter. They were playing draw poker. O'Hara was not surprised to see that most of the stakes—gold specie and greenbacks—were in front of Colfax.

Casually, O'Hara approached the table and stopped

behind an empty chair next to the portly man, just as Colfax claimed a pot with four treys. He said, "Good evening, gentlemen."

Colfax greeted him unctuously, asked if he were enjoying the voyage thus far. O'Hara said he was, and observed that the gambler seemed to be enjoying it too, judging from the stack of legal tender before him. Colfax just smiled. But the portly man said in grumbling tones, "I should damned well say so. He has been taking my money for three solid hours."

"Aye? That long?"

"Since just after dinner."

"Ye've been playing without pause since then?"

"Nearly so," the newspaperman said. Through the tendrils of smoke from his cigar, he studied O'Hara with mild blue eyes. "Why do you ask, sir?"

"Oh, I was thinking I saw Mr. Colfax up on the weather deck about an hour ago. Near the pilothouse."

"You must have mistaken someone else for me," Colfax said. Now that the draw game had been momentarily suspended, he had produced a handful of war-issue coins and begun to toy with them as he had done at Long Wharf. "I did leave the table for a few minutes about an hour ago, but only to use the lavatory. I haven't been on the weather deck at all this trip."

O'Hara saw no advantage in pressing the matter. He pretended to notice for the first time the one-cent pieces Colfax was shuffling. "Lucky coins, Mr. Colfax?"

"These? Why, yes. I won a sackful of them on a wager once and my luck has been good ever since." Disarming smile. "Gamblers are superstitious about such things, you know."

"Ye don't see many coins like that in California."

"True. They are practically worthless out here."

"So worthless," the reporter said, "that I have seen them

used to decorate various leather goods."

The portly man said irritably, "To hell with lucky coins and such nonsense. Are we going to play poker or have a gabfest?"

"Poker, by all means," Colfax said. He slipped the war-issue cents into a pocket of his Prince Albert and reached for the cards. His interest in O'Hara seemed to have vanished.

The reporter, however, was still looking at him with curiosity. "Perhaps you'd care to join us?"

O'Hara declined, saying he had never had any luck with the pasteboards. Then he left the saloon and went in search of the *Delta Star*'s purser. It took him ten minutes to find the man, and thirty seconds to learn that John A. Colfax did not have a stateroom either in the texas or on the deckhouse. The purser, who knew Colfax as a regular passenger, said wryly that the gambler would spend the entire voyage in the Gentlemen's Saloon, having gullible citizens for a ride.

O'Hara returned to the saloon, this time to avail himself of the liquor buffet. He ordered a shot of rye from a bartender who owned a resplendent handlebar moustache, and tossed it down without his customary enjoyment. Immediately he ordered another.

Colfax might well be his man; there was the war-issue coin he'd found under the pilothouse stove, and the fact that Colfax had left the poker game at about the time of the robbery. And yet . . . what could he have done with the gold? The weight of forty thousand in dust was considerable; he could not very well carry it in his pockets. He had been gone from the poker game long enough to commit the robbery, perhaps, but hardly long enough to have also hidden the spoils.

There were other factors weighing against Colfax, too. One: gentlemen gamblers made considerable sums of money at their trade; they seldom found it necessary to resort to baser thievery. Two: how could Colfax, while sitting here in the saloon, have known when only one man would be present in the pilothouse? An accomplice might have been on watch—but if there were such a second party, why hadn't he committed the robbery himself?

O'Hara scowled, put away his second rye. If Colfax wasn't the culprit, then who was? And what was the significance of the coin he had found in the pilothouse?

Perhaps the coin had no significance at all; but his instincts told him it did, and he had always trusted his instincts. If not to Colfax, then to whom did it point? Answer: to no one, and to everyone. Even though war-issue cents were uncommon in California, at least half a dozen men presently on board might have one or two in their pockets.

A remark passed by the newspaperman came back to him: such coins were used to decorate various leather goods. Aye, that was a possibility. If the guilty man had been wearing a holster or vest or some other article adorned with the cent pieces, one might have popped loose unnoticed.

O'Hara slid the coin from his pocket and examined it carefully. There were small scratches on its surface that might have been made by stud fasteners, but he couldn't be sure. The scratches might also have been caused by any one of a hundred other means—and the coin could still belong to John A. Colfax.

Returning it to his vest pocket, O'Hara considered the idea of conducting a search for a man wearing leather ornamented with bronze war coins. And dismissed it immediately as folly. He could roam the *Delta Star* all night and not encounter even two-thirds of the passengers. Or he might find someone wearing such an article who would turn out to be completely innocent. And what if the robber had discovered the loss of the coin and chucked the article overboard?

Frustration began to assail him now. But it did not dull his determination. If any man aboard the *Delta Star* could fetch up both the thief and the gold before the packet reached Stockton, that man was Fergus O'Hara; and by damn, if such were humanly possible, he meant to do it!

He left the saloon again and went up to the pilothouse. Bridgeman was alone at the wheel. "What news, O'Hara?" he asked.

"None as yet. Would ye know where the captain is?"

Bridgeman shook his head. "Young fool Chadwick was feeling dizzy from that blow on the head; the captain took him to his quarters just after you and your wife left, and then went to make his inquiries. I expect he's still making 'em."

O'Hara sat on the red plush sofa, packed and lighted his pipe, and let his mind drift along various channels. After a time something in his memory flickered like a guttering candle—and then died before he could steady the flame. When he was unable to rekindle the flame he roared forth with a venomous ten-jointed oath that startled even Bridgeman.

Presently the captain returned to the pilothouse. He and O'Hara exchanged identical expectant looks, which immediately told each that the other had uncovered nothing of significance. Verbal confirmation of this was brief, after which the captain said bleakly, "The prospects are grim, Mr. O'Hara. Grim, indeed."

"We've not yet come into Stockton," O'Hara reminded him.

The captain sighed. "We have no idea of who is guilty, thus no idea of where to find the gold . . . if in fact it is still on board. We haven't the manpower for a search of packet and passengers before our arrival. And afterward—I don't see how we can hope to hold everyone on board while the authorities are summoned and a search mounted. Miners are a hotheaded lot; so are those Irish militiamen. We would likely have a riot on our hands."

O'Hara had nothing more to say. By all the saints, he was not yet ready to admit defeat. He bid the captain and Bridgeman good night, and spent the next hour prowling the decks and cudgeling his brain. It seemed to him that he had seen and heard enough since the robbery to know who it was he was after and where the missing gold could be found. If only he could bring forth one scrap of this knowledge from his memory, he was certain the others would follow . . .

Maddeningly, however, no scrap was forthcoming. Not while he prowled the decks, not after he returned to his stateroom (Hattie, he was relieved to find, was already fast asleep)—and not when the first light of dawn crept into the sky beyond the window.

When the *Delta Star* came out of one of the snakelike bends in the river and started down the last long reach to Stockton, O'Hara was standing with Hattie at the starboard deckhouse rail. It was just past seven-thirty—a spring-crisp, cloudless St. Patrick's Day morning—and the steamer would dock in another thirty minutes.

O'Hara was in a foul humor: three-quarters frustration and one-quarter lack of sleep. He had left the stateroom at six o'clock and gone up to the pilothouse and found the captain, Bridgeman, and Chadwick drinking coffee thickened with molasses. They had nothing to tell him. And their humors had been no better than his; it seemed that as a result of O'Hara's failure to perform as advertised, he had fallen out of favor with them.

Staring down at the slow-moving waters frothed by the sidewheel, he told himself for the thousandth time: Ye've got the answer, ye know ye do. Think, lad! Dredge it up before it's too late . . .

A voice beside him said, "Fine morning, isn't it?"

Irritably O'Hara turned his head and found himself looking into the cheerfully smiling visage of the Nevada newspaperman. The bushy-haired lad's eyes were red-veined from a long night in the Gentlemen's Saloon, but this did not seem to have had any effect on his disposition.

O'Hara grunted. "Is it?" he said grumpily. "Ye sound as if ye have cause for rejoicing. Did ye win a hatful of specie from the gambler Colfax last night?"

"Unfortunately, no. I lost a fair sum, as a matter of fact. Gambling is one of my sadder vices, along with a fondness for the social drink. But then, a man may have no bad habits and have worse."

O'Hara grunted again and looked out over the broad, yellowish land of the San Joaquin Valley.

The reporter's gaze was on the river. "Clear as a mirror, isn't it?" he said nostalgically. "Not at all like the Mississippi. I remember when I was a boy . . ."

O'Hara had jerked upright, into a posture as rigid as an obelisk. He stood that way for several seconds. Then he said explosively, "In the name of Patrick and all the saints!"

Hattie said with alarm in her voice, "Fergus, what is it?"

O'Hara grinned at her, swung around to the newspaperman and clapped him exuberantly on the shoulder. "Lad, it may yet be a fine a morning. It may yet be, indeed."

He told Hattie to wait there for him, left her and the bewildered reporter at the rail, and hurried down to the aft stairway. On the weather deck, he moved aft of the texas and stopped before the gallows frame.

There was no one in the immediate vicinity. O'Hara stepped up close to the frame and eased his head and both arms inside the vent opening, avoiding the machinery of the massive walking-beam. Heat and the heavy odor of cylinder oil assailed him; the throb of the piston was almost deafening.

With his left hand he felt along the interior wall of the frame, his fingertips encountering a greasy build-up of oil and dust. It was only a few seconds before they located a metal hook screwed into the wood. A new hook, free of grease; he was able to determine that by touching it with the clean fingers of his right hand. Nothing was suspended from the hook, but O'Hara was now certain that something had been during most of the night.

He was also certain that he knew where it could be found at this very moment.

When he withdrew his head and arms from the vent opening, grease stained his hands and his coat and shirt sleeves, and he was sweating from the heat. He used his handkerchief, then hastened across to enter the texas. There were identifying plates screwed to the doors of the officers' cabins; he stopped before the one he wanted, drew his coat away from his revolver and laid the fingers of his right hand on its grip. With his left hand he rapped on the door panel.

There was no response.

He knocked again, waited, then took out his pocket knife. The door latch yielded in short order to rapid manipulations with one of the blades. He slipped inside and shut the door behind him.

A brief look around convinced him that the most likely hiding place was a dark corner formed by the single bunkbed and an open-topped wooden tool carrier. And that in fact was where he found what he was looking for: a wide leather belt ornamented with bronze war-issue coins, and a greasy calfskin grip. He drew the bag out, worked at the locked catch with his knife, and got it open.

The missing gold was inside, in two-score small pouches.

O'Hara looked at the sacks for several seconds, smiling. Then he found himself thinking of the captain, and of the bank in Stockton that urgently awaited the consignment. He sobered, shook himself mentally. This was neither the time nor the place for rumination; there was still much to be done. He refastened the grip, hefted it, and started to rise.

Scraping noise on the deck outside. Then the cabin door burst open, and the man whose quarters these were, the man who had stolen the gold, stood framed in the opening.

Chadwick, the cub pilot.

Recognition darkened his face with the blood of rage. He growled, "So you found out, did you? You damned Pinkerton meddler!" And he launched himself across the cabin.

O'Hara moved to draw his revolver too late. By then Chadwick was on him. The young pilot's shoulder struck the carpetbag that O'Hara thrust up defensively, sandwiched it between them as they went crashing into the larboard bulkhead. The impact broke them apart. O'Hara spilled sideways across the bunk, with the grip between his legs, and cracked his head on the rounded projection of wood that served as headboard. An eruption of pain blurred his vision, kept him from reacting as quickly as he might have. Chadwick was on him again before he could disengage himself from the bag.

A wild blow grazed the side of O'Hara's head. He threw up a forearm, succeeded in warding off a second blow but not a third. That one connected solidly with his jaw, and his vision went cockeyed again.

He was still conscious, but he seemed to have momentarily lost all power of movement. The flailing weight that was Chadwick lifted from him. There were scuffling sounds, then the sharp running slap of boots receding across the cabin and on the deck outside.

O'Hara's jaw and the back of his head began a simultaneous and painful throbbing; at the same time strength seemed to flow back into his arms and legs. Shaking his head to clear his vision, he swung off the bunk and let loose with a many-jointed oath that even his grandfather, who had always sworn he could out-cuss Old Nick himself, would have been proud to call his own. When he could see again he realized that Chadwick had caught up the calfskin grip and taken it with him. He hobbled to the door and turned to larboard out of it, the way the running steps had gone.

Chadwick, hampered by the weight and bulk of the grip, was at the bottom of the aft stairway when O'Hara reached the top. He glanced upward, saw O'Hara, and began to race frantically toward the nearby main-deck staircase. He banged into passengers, scattering them; whirled a fat woman around like a ballerina executing a pirouette and sent the reticule she had been carrying over the rail into the river.

Men commenced calling in angry voices and milling about as O'Hara tumbled down the stairs to the deckhouse. A bearded, red-shirted miner stepped into Chadwick's path at the top of the main-deck stairway; without slowing, the cub pilot bowled him over as if he were a giant ninepin and went down the stairs in a headlong dash. O'Hara lurched through the confusion of passengers and descended after him, cursing eloquently all the while.

Chadwick shoved two startled Chinese out of the way at the foot of the stairs and raced toward the taffrail, looking back over his shoulder. The bloody fool was going to jump into the river, O'Hara thought. And when he did, the weight of the gold would take both him and the bag straight to the bottom—

All at once O'Hara became aware that there were not many passengers inhabiting the aft section of the main deck, when there should have been a clotted mass of them. Some of those who were present had heard the commotion on the upper deck and been drawn to the staircase; the rest were split into two groups, one lining the larboard rail and the other lining the starboard, and their attention was held by a different spectacle. Some were murmuring excitedly; others looked amused; still others wore apprehensive expressions. The center section of the deck opposite the taffrail was completely cleared.

The reason for this was that a small, rusted, and very old half-pounder had been set up on wooden chocks at the taffrail, aimed downriver like an impolitely pointing finger.

Beside the cannon was a keg of black powder and a charred-looking ramrod.

And surrounding the cannon were the Mulrooney Guards, one of whom held a firebrand poised above the fuse vent and all of whom were now loudly singing "The Wearing of the Green."

O'Hara knew in that moment what it was the Mulrooneys had had secreted inside their wooden crate, and why they had been so anxious to get it aboard without having the contents examined; and he knew the meaning of Billy Culligan's remark about planning to start off St. Patrick's day with a mighty salute. He stopped running and opened his mouth to shout at Chadwick, who was still fleeing and still looking back over his shoulder. He could not recall afterward if he actually did shout or not; if so, it was akin to whispering in a thunderstorm.

The Mulrooney cannoneer touched off the fuse. The other Mulrooney Guards scattered, still singing. The watching passengers huddled farther back, some averting their eyes. Chadwick kept on running toward the taffrail.

And the cannon, as well as the keg of black powder, promptly blew up.

The *Delta Star* lurched and rolled with the sudden concussion. A great sweeping cloud of sulfurous black smoke enveloped the riverboat. O'Hara caught hold of one of the uprights in the starboard rail and clung to it, coughing and choking. Too much black powder and not enough bracing, he thought. Then he thought: I hope Hattie had the good sense to stay where she was on the deckhouse.

The steamer was in a state of bedlam: everyone on each of the three decks screaming or shouting. Some of the passengers thought a boiler had exploded, a common steamboat hazard. When the smoke finally began to dissipate, O'Hara looked in the direction of the center taffrail and discovered that most of it, like the cannon, was missing. The deck in that area was blackened and scarred, some of the boarding torn into splinters.

But there did not seem to have been any casualties. A few passengers had received minor injuries, most of them Mulrooney Guards, and several were speckled with black soot. No one had fallen overboard. Even Chadwick had miraculously managed to survive the concussion, despite his proximity to the cannon when it and the powder keg had gone up. He was moaning feebly and moving his arms and legs, looking like a bedraggled chimney sweep, when O'Hara reached his side.

The grip containing the gold had fared somewhat better. Chadwick had been shielding it with his body at the moment of the blast, and while it was torn open and the leather pouches scattered about, most of the sacks were intact. One or two had split open, and particles of gold dust glittered in the sooty air. The preponderance of passengers were too concerned with their own welfare to notice; those who did stared with disbelief but kept their distance, for no sooner had O'Hara reached Chadwick than the captain and half a dozen of the deck crew arrived.

"Chadwick?" the captain said in amazement. "*Chadwick's* the thief?"

"Aye, he's the one."

"But . . . what happened? What was he doing here with the gold?"

"I was chasing him, the spalpeen."

"You were? Then . . . you knew of his guilt before the explosion? How?"

"I'll explain it all to ye later," O'Hara said. "Right now there's me wife to consider."

He left the bewildered captain and his crew to attend to Chadwick and the gold, and went to find Hattie.

Shortly past nine, an hour after the *Delta Star* had docked at the foot of Stockton's Center Street, O'Hara stood with Hattie and a group of men on the landing. He wore his last clean suit, a broadcloth, and a bright green tie in honor of St. Patrick's Day. The others, clustered around him, were Bridgeman, the captain, the Nevada reporter, a hawkish man who was Stockton's sheriff, and two officials of the California Merchants Bank. Chadwick had been removed to the local jail in the company of a pair of deputies and a doctor. The Mulrooney Guards, after medical treatment, a severe reprimand, and a promise to pay all damages to the packet, had been released to continue their merrymaking in Green Park.

The captain was saying, "We are all deeply indebted to you, Mr. O'Hara. It would have been a black day if Chadwick had succeeded in escaping with the gold—a black day for us all."

"I only did me duty," O'Hara said solemnly.

"It is unfortunate that the California Merchants Bank cannot offer you a reward," one of the bank officials said. "However, we are not a wealthy concern, as our urgent need for the consignment of dust attests. But I don't suppose you could accept a reward in any case; the Pinkertons never do, I'm told."

"Aye, that's true."

Bridgeman said, "Will you explain now how you knew Chadwick was the culprit? And how he accomplished the theft? He refused to confess, you know."

O'Hara nodded. He told them of finding the war-issue coin under the pilothouse stove; his early suspicions of the gambler, Colfax; the reporter's remark that such coins were being used in California to decorate leather goods; his growing certainty that he had seen and heard enough to piece together the truth, and yet his maddening inability to cudgel forth the necessary scraps from his memory.

"It wasn't until this morning that the doors in me mind finally opened," he said. He looked at the newspaperman. "It was this gentleman that gave me the key."

The reporter was surprised. "*I* gave you the key?"

"Ye did," O'Hara told him. "Ye said of the river: *Clear as a mirror, isn't it?* Do ye remember saying that, while we were together at the rail?"

"I do. But I don't see—"

"It was the word *mirror,*" O'Hara said. "It caused me to think of reflection, and all at once I was recalling how I'd been able to see me own image in the pilothouse windshield soon after the robbery. Yet Chadwick claimed he was sitting in the pilot's seat when he heard the door open just before he was struck, and that he didn't turn because he thought it was the captain and Mr. Bridgeman returning from supper. But if

I was able to see *me* reflection in the glass, Chadwick would sure have been able to see his—and anybody creeping up behind him.

"Then I recalled something else: Chadwick had his coat buttoned when I first entered the pilothouse, on a warm night like the last. Why? And why did his trousers look so baggy, as though they might fall down?

"Well, then, the answer was this: After Chadwick broke open the safe and the strongbox, his problem was what to do with the gold. He couldn't risk a trip to his quarters while he was alone in the pilothouse; he might be seen, and there was also the possibility that the *Delta Star* would run into a bar or snag if she slipped off course. D'ye recall saying it was a miracle such hadn't happened, Captain, thinking as ye were then that Chadwick had been unconscious for some time?"

The captain said he did.

"So Chadwick had to have the gold on his person," O'Hara said, "when you and Mr. Bridgeman found him, and when Hattie and I entered soon afterward. He couldn't have removed it until later, when he claimed to be feeling dizzy and you escorted him to his cabin. That, now, is the significance of the buttoned coat and the baggy trousers.

"What he must have done was to take off his belt, the wide one decorated with war-issue coins that I found in his cabin, and use it to strap the gold pouches above his waist—a makeshift money belt, ye see. He was in such a rush, for fear of being found out, that he failed to notice when one of the coins popped loose and rolled under the stove.

"Once he had the pouches secured, he waited until he heard Mr. Bridgeman and the captain returning, the while tending to his piloting duties; then he lay down on the floor and pretended to've been knocked senseless. He kept his loose coat buttoned for fear someone would notice the thickness about his upper middle, and that he was no longer wearing his belt in its proper place; and he kept hitching up his trousers because he wasn't wearing the belt in its proper place."

Hattie took her husband's arm. "Fergus, what did Chadwick do with the gold afterward? Did he have it hidden in his quarters all along?"

"No, me lady. I expect he was afraid of a search, so first chance he had he put the gold into the calfskin grip and then hung the grip from a metal hook inside the gallows frame."

The Stockton sheriff asked, "How could you possibly have deduced that fact?"

"While in the pilothouse after the robbery," O'Hara said, "I noticed that Chadwick's coat was soiled with dust and soot from his lying on the floor. But it also showed streaks of grease, which couldn't have come from the floor. When the other pieces fell into place this morning, I reasoned that he might have picked up the grease marks while making preparations to hide the gold. My consideration then was that he'd have wanted a place close to his quarters, and the only such place with grease about it was the gallows frame. The hook I discovered inside was new and free of grease; Chadwick, therefore, must have put it there only recently—tonight, in fact, thus accounting for the grease on his coat."

"Amazing detective work," the reporter said, "simply amazing."

Everyone else agreed.

"You really are a fine detective, Fergus O'Hara," Hattie said. "Amazing, indeed."

O'Hara said nothing. Now that they were five minutes parted from the others, walking alone together along

Stockton's dusty main street, he had begun scowling and grumbling to himself.

Hattie ventured, "It's a splendid, sunny St. Patrick's Day. Shall we join the festivities in Green Park?"

"We've nothing to celebrate," O'Hara muttered.

"Still thinking about the gold, are you?"

"And what else would I be thinking about?" he said. "Fine detective—faugh! Some consolation *that* is!"

It was Hattie's turn to be silent.

O'Hara wondered sourly what those lads back at the landing would say if they knew the truth of the matter: That he was no more a Pinkerton operative than were the Mulrooney Guards. That he had only been impersonating one toward his own ends, in this case and others since he had taken the railroad pass and letter of introduction off the chap in Saint Louis the previous year—the Pinkerton chap who'd foolishly believed he was taking O'Hara to jail. That he had wanted the missing pouches of gold for himself and Hattie. And that he, Fergus O'Hara, was the finest *confidence man* in these sovereign United States, come to Stockton, California, to have for a ride a banker who intended to cheat the government by buying up Indian land.

Well, those lads would never know any of this, because he had duped them all—brilliantly, as always. And for nothing. Nothing!

He moaned aloud, "Forty thousand in gold, Hattie. Forty thousand that I was holding in me hands, clutched fair to me black heart, when that rascal Chadwick burst in on me. Two more minutes, just two more minutes . . ."

"It was Providence," she said. "You were never meant to have that gold, Fergus."

"What d'ye mean? The field was white for the sickle—"

"Not a bit of that," Hattie said. "And if you'll be truthful with yourself, you'll admit you enjoyed every minute of your play-acting of a detective; every minute of the explaining just now of your brilliant deductions."

"I didn't," O'Hara lied weakly. "I hate detectives . . ."

"Bosh. I'm glad the gold went to its rightful owners, and you should be too because your heart is about as black as this sunny morning. You've only stolen from dishonest men in all the time I've known you. Why, if you *had* succeeded in filching the gold, you'd have begun despising yourself sooner than you realize—not only because it belongs to honest citizens but because you would have committed the crime on St. Patrick's Day. If you stop to consider it, you wouldn't commit *any* crime on St. Pat's Day, now would you?"

O'Hara grumbled and glowered, but he was remembering his thoughts in Chadwick's cabin, when he had held the gold in his hands—thoughts of the captain's reputation and possible loss of position, and of the urgent need of the new branch bank in Stockton. He was not at all sure, now, that he would have kept the pouches if Chadwick had not burst in on him. He might well have returned them to the captain. Confound it, that was just what he would have done.

Hattie was right about St. Pat's Day, too. He would not feel decent if he committed a crime on—

Abruptly, he stopped walking. Then he put down their luggage and said, "You wait here, me lady. There's something that needs doing before we set off for Green Park."

Before Hattie could speak, he was on his way through clattering wagons and carriages to where a towheaded boy was scuffling with a mongrel dog. He halted before the boy. "Now then, lad, how would ye like to have a dollar for twenty minutes good work?"

The boy's eyes grew wide. "What do I have to do, mister?"

O'Hara removed from the inside pocket of his coat an expensive gold American Horologe watch, which happened to be in his possession as the result of a momentary lapse in good sense and fingers made nimble during his misspent youth in New Orleans. He extended it to the boy.

"Take this down to the *Delta Star* steamboat and look about for a tall gentleman with a mustache and a fine head of bushy hair, a newspaperman from Nevada. When ye've found him, give him the watch and tell him Mr. Fergus O'Hara came upon it, is returning it, and wishes him a happy St. Patrick's Day."

"What's his name, mister?" the boy asked. "It'll help me find him quicker."

O'Hara could not seem to recall it, if he had ever heard it in the first place. He took the watch again, opened the hunting-style case, and saw that a name had been etched in flowing script on the dustcover. He handed the watch back to the boy.

"Clemens, it is," O'Hara said then. "A Mr. Samuel Langhorne Clemens . . ."

Chip

John Valarian felt as he always did when he came to St. Ives Academy—a little awkward and uncomfortable, as if he didn't really belong in a place like this. St. Ives was one of the most exclusive, expensive boys' schools on the east coast, but that wasn't the reason; he'd picked it out himself, over Andrea's objections, when Peter reached his eighth birthday two years ago. The wooded country setting and hundred-year-old stone buildings weren't the reason, either. It was what the school represented, the atmosphere you felt as soon as you entered the grounds. Knowledge. Good breeding. Status. Class.

Well, maybe he *didn't* belong here. He'd come out of the city slums, had to fight for every rung on his way up the ladder. He hadn't had much schooling, still had trouble reading. And he'd never been able to polish off all his rough edges. That was one of the reasons he was determined to give his son the best education money could buy.

He climbed the worn stone steps of the administration building, gave his name to the lobby receptionist. She directed him up another flight of stairs to the headmaster's office. He'd been there once before, on the day he'd brought Peter here for enrollment, but he didn't remember much about it except that he'd been deeply impressed. This was only his third visit to St. Ives in three years—just two short ones before today. It made him feel bad, neglectful, thinking about it now. He'd intended to come more often, particularly for the father-son days, but some business matter always got in the way. Business ruled him. He didn't like it sometimes, but that was the way it was. Some things you couldn't change no matter what.

The headmaster kept him waiting less than five minutes. His name was Locklear. Late fifties, silver-haired, looked exactly like you'd expect the head of St. Ives Academy to look. When they were alone in his private office, Locklear shook hands gravely and said, "Thank you for coming, Mr. Valarian. Please sit down."

He perched on the edge of a maroon leather chair, now tense and on guard as well as uncomfortable. The way he'd felt when he got sent to the principal's office in public school. He didn't know what to do with his hands, finally slid them down tight over his knees. His gaze roamed the office. Nice. Books everywhere, a big illuminated globe on a wooden stand, a desk that had to be pure Philippine mahogany, a bank of windows that looked out over the central quadrangle and rolling lawns beyond. Impressive, all right. He wouldn't mind having a desk like that one himself.

He waited until Locklear was seated behind it before he said, "This trouble with my son. It must be pretty serious if you couldn't talk about it on the phone."

"I'm afraid it is. Quite serious."

"Bad grades or what?"

"No. Chip is extremely bright, and his grades—"

"Peter."

"Ah, yes, of course."

"His mother calls him that. I don't."

"He seems to prefer it."

"His name is Peter. Chip sounds . . . ordinary."

"Your son is anything but ordinary, Mr. Valarian."

The way the headmaster said that tightened him up even

more. "What's going on here?" he demanded. "What's Peter done?"

"We're not absolutely certain he's responsible for any of the . . . incidents. I should make that clear at the outset. However, the circumstantial evidence is considerable and points to no one else."

Incidents. Circumstantial evidence. "Get to the point, Mr. Locklear. What do you *think* he did?"

The headmaster leaned forward, made a steeple of his fingertips. He seemed to be hiding behind it as he said, "There have been a series of thefts in Chip's . . . in Peter's dormitory, beginning several weeks ago. Small amounts of cash pilfered from the rooms of nearly a dozen different boys."

"My son's not a thief."

"I sincerely hope that's so. But as I said, the circumstantial evidence—"

"Why would he steal money? He's got plenty of his own—I send him more than he can spend every month."

"I can't answer your question. I wish I could."

"You ask him about the thefts?"

"Yes."

"And?"

"He denies taking any money."

"All right then," Valarian said. "If he says he didn't do it, then he didn't do it."

"Two of the victims saw him coming out of their rooms immediately before they discovered missing sums."

"And you believe these kids over my son."

"Given the other circumstances, we have no choice."

"What other circumstances?"

"Chip has been involved in—"

"Peter."

"I'm sorry, yes, Peter. He has been involved in several

physical altercations recently. Last week one of the boys he attacked suffered a broken nose."

"Attacked? How do you know he did the attacking?"

"There were witnesses," Locklear said. "To that assault and to the others. In each case, they swore Peter was the aggressor."

The office seemed to have grown too warm; Valarian could feel himself starting to sweat. "He's a little aggressive, I admit that. Always has been. A lot of kids his age—"

"His behavior goes beyond simple aggression, I'm afraid. I can only describe it as bullying to the point of terrorizing."

"Come on, now. I don't believe that."

"Nevertheless, it's true. If you'd care to talk to his teachers, his classmates . . ."

Valarian shook his head. After a time he said, "If this has been going on for a while, why didn't you let me know before?"

"At first the incidents were isolated, and without proof that Peter was responsible for the thefts . . . well, we try to give our young men the benefit of the doubt whenever possible. But as they grew more frequent, more violent, I *did* inform you of the problem. Twice by letter, once in a message when I couldn't reach you by phone at your office."

He stared at the headmaster, but it was only a few seconds before his disbelief faded and he lowered his gaze. Two letters, one phone call. Dimly he remembered getting one of the letters, reading it, dismissing it as unimportant because he was in the middle of a big transaction with the Chicago office. The other letter . . . misplaced, inadvertently thrown out or filed. The phone call . . . dozens came in every day, he had two secretaries screening them and taking messages, and sometimes the messages didn't get delivered.

He didn't know what to say. He sat there sweating, feeling like a fool.

"Last evening there was another occurrence," Locklear said, "the most serious of all. That is why I called this morning and insisted on speaking to you in person. We can't prove that your son is responsible, but given what we do know we can hardly come to another conclusion."

"What occurrence? What happened last night?"

"Someone," Locklear said carefully, "set fire to our gymnasium."

"Set fire—my God."

"Fortunately it was discovered in time to prevent the fire from burning out of control and destroying the entire facility, but it did cause several thousand dollars' damage."

"What makes you think Peter set it?"

"He had an argument with his physical education instructor yesterday afternoon. He became quite abusive and made thinly veiled threats. It was in the instructor's office that kerosene was poured and the fire set."

Valarian opened his mouth, clicked it shut again. He couldn't seem to think clearly now. Too damn quiet in there; he could hear a clock ticking somewhere. He broke the silence in a voice that sounded like a stranger's.

"What're you going to do? Expel him? Is that why you got me up here?"

"Believe me, Mr. Valarian, it pains me to say this, but yes, that is the board's decision. For the welfare of St. Ives Academy and the other students. Surely you can understand—"

"Oh, I understand," Valarian said bitterly. "You bet I understand."

"Peter will be permitted to remain here until the end of the week, under supervision, if you require time to make other arrangements for him. Of course, if you'd rather he leave with you this afternoon . . ."

Valarian got jerkily to his feet. "I want to talk to my son. Now."

"Yes, naturally. I sent for him earlier and he's waiting in one of the rooms just down the hall."

He had to fight his anger as he followed the headmaster to where Peter was waiting. He felt like hitting something or somebody. Not the boy, he'd never laid a hand on him and never would. Not Locklear, either. Somebody. Himself, maybe.

Locklear stopped before a closed door. He said somberly, "I'll await you in my office, Mr. Valarian," and left him there alone.

He hesitated before going in, to calm down and work out how he was going to handle this. All right. He took a couple of heavy breaths and opened the door.

The boy was sitting on a straightback chair—not doing anything, just sitting there like a statue. When he saw his father he got slowly to his feet and stood with his arms down at his sides. No smile, nothing but a blank stare. He looked older than ten. Big for his age, lean but wide through the shoulders. *He looks like I did at that age,* Valarian thought. *He looks just like me.*

"Hello, Peter."

"Chip," the boy said in a voice as blank as his stare. "You know I prefer Chip, Papa."

"Your name is Peter. I prefer Peter."

Valarian crossed the room to him. The boy put out his hand, but on impulse Valarian bent and caught his shoulders and hugged him. It was like hugging a piece of stone. Valarian let go of him, stepped back.

"I just had a long talk with your headmaster," he said.

"Those thefts, the fire yesterday . . . he says it was you."

"I know."

"Well? Was it?"

"No, Papa."

"Don't lie to me. If you did all that . . ."

"I didn't. I didn't do anything."

"They're kicking you out of St. Ives. They wouldn't do that if they weren't sure it was you."

"I don't care."

"You don't care you're being expelled?"

"I don't like it here anymore. I don't care what the headmaster or the teachers or the other kids think. I don't care what anybody thinks about me." Funny little smile. "Except you, Papa."

"All right," Valarian said. "Look me in the eyes and tell me the truth. *Did* you steal money, set that fire?"

"I already told you I didn't."

"In my eyes. Up close."

The boy stepped forward and looked up at him squarely. "No, Papa, I didn't," he said.

In the car on the way back to the city he kept seeing Peter's eyes staring into his. He couldn't get them out of his mind. What he'd seen there shining deep and dark . . . it must've been there all along. How could he have missed it before? It had made him feel cold all over; made him want nothing more to do with his son today, tell Locklear he'd send somebody to pick up the boy at the end of the week and then get out of there fast. Now, remembering, it made him shudder.

Lugo was looking at him in the rear view mirror. "Something wrong, Mr. Valarian?"

At any other time he'd have said no and let it go at that. But now he heard himself say, "It's my son. He got into some trouble. That's why I had to go to the school."

"All taken care of now?"

"No. They're throwing him out."

"No kidding? That's too bad."

"Is it?" Then he said, "His name's Peter, but his mother calls him Chip. She says he's like me, a chip off the same block. He likes the name, he thinks it fits him too. But I don't like it."

"How come?"

"I don't want him to be like me, I wanted him to grow up better than me. Better in every way. That's why I sent him to St. Ives. You understand?"

Lugo said, "Yes, sir," but they were just words. Lugo was his driver, his bodyguard, his strongarm man; all Lugo understood was how to steer a limo, how to serve the mob with muscle or a gun.

"I don't want him in my business," he said. "I don't want him to be another John Valarian."

"But now you think maybe he will be?"

"No, that's not what I think." Valarian crossed himself, picturing those bright, cold eyes. "I think he's gonna be a hell of a lot worse."

Opportunity

Coretti and I went to check the thing out.

The call had come in to the captain of detectives at eight thirty-five from an occasionally reliable department informant named Scully. We were logging reports in the squad room when the word came down. It had been a quiet night, like you can get in early winter, the sound of the wind and a thin rain snapping at the windows, and none of us relished the thought of leaving the warmth of the squad room. So we matched coins with the two other teams of inspectors on the four-to-midnight swing to see who would take the squeal. Coretti and I lost.

It didn't sound like much, but then you never know. A parlor collector for a string of bookie joints in Southern California had vanished with a substantial amount of weekend receipts. Scully didn't know how much, but since the betting had been unusually heavy at Caliente on Saturday his guess was six figures. Scully's tip, uncorroborated and filtering north on the grapevine, was that this Feldstein had beat it to San Francisco and gone into hiding in a tenement hotel near Hunters Point. The captain thought we ought to run a check.

Coretti and I rode the elevator down to the garage in the basement of the Hall of Justice and signed a check-out slip for an unmarked sedan. We drove out into the frigid, drizzling San Francisco night. The hotel Scully had named was off Third Street, in an area that was primarily industrial. At least it wouldn't be a long ride.

Neither of us had much to say. We'd been partners a long time and we didn't need a lot of conversation. The heater in the sedan made labored whirring sounds and threw nothing but cold air against our feet.

Coretti picked up Third at Townsend, followed it out over China Basin. I lit a cigarette as we passed over the bridge, and as soon as I exhaled smoke the pain in my stomach almost doubled me over on the seat. I jammed my hand under my breastbone and held it there, waiting for the sharpness of the seizure to subside so I could breathe again.

"Arne," Coretti said, "you all right?"

I fumbled out the bottle of prescription painkiller, swallowed some of it. It was strong stuff and it worked quickly. Pretty soon I said, "Yeah. Okay now."

"The ulcer again?"

"What else," I said.

"You take that medicine like it was candy. Doesn't seem to be helping much."

"It's mostly for the pain. Doc says I've got to have an operation. He's afraid the thing will rupture."

"So when you going in, Arne?"

"I'm not."

He gave me a sharp look. "Why not? Man, a perforated ulcer can kill you."

"I can't afford an operation right now. I'm up to my ass in bills. You've got a family, Bob. You know how it is."

"Yeah, I know how it is."

"Maybe next summer," I said. "The car loan'll be paid off then."

"Does the captain know how bad the ulcer is?"

"No, and don't you tell him. I haven't even told my wife yet."

"You can't keep it a secret, Arne," Coretti said. "Some of

the boys are beginning to notice these spasms you get. Captain's bound to find out. It'd be a lot easier if you told him yourself."

"You know as well as I do what it means if I tell him—disability. I can barely live on what I make now, Bob. How can I live on disability pay?"

"Just the same, you can't keep on this way. You look worn out. If you won't go in for the operation, why not take some time off at least? You've got sick leave coming."

"Maybe you're right. I could use a rest."

"Sure I'm right," Coretti said. "And if I were you, I'd do some serious thinking about that operation. Talk it over with Gerry, too."

"Some R&R is all I need for now. I'll tell Gerry when the time comes."

"When you can't put the operation off any longer, you mean."

"Let's just drop the subject, okay? I don't feel like talking anymore right now."

It had begun to rain in earnest now. Coretti put the wipers on high. The bitter cold wind blowing in across the Bay whipped sheets of water across the windshield, and you could hear it howling at the windows of the sedan. I sat with my legs straight out in front of me to ease the gnawing in my stomach. I wished I were home in bed with Gerry's warm little body against my back.

Coretti made a left-hand turn, drove two blocks, made another turn. The hotel stood between a storage warehouse for an interstate truck line and an iron foundry, midway on the block. It was a three-story wooden affair, well over half a century old—a shambling reminder of another era. A narrow alley separated it from the iron foundry on the right.

We left the sedan's semi-warmth and hurried inside. The

rain was like ice on the back of my neck. The lobby stank of age-must and disinfectant, the smell of death wrapped in formaldehyde. It was small, dark, sparsely furnished; no elevator, just a staircase leading to the upper floors. A desk paralleled the wall on the right. No one was behind it.

"Nice place," Coretti said, glancing around. "Homey, you know?"

From behind a closed door next to the desk came the sounds of a TV, the volume turned up high. We went over there and I knocked and pretty soon a rheumy-looking old character in a T-shirt and baggy trousers held up by three-inch-wide suspenders peered out at us.

"You the night clerk?" I asked him.

"Yep. Night clerk, night manager, handyman." He peered harder. "You fellas looking for a room? If you are, I got to tell you we—"

"Police," I said. We showed him our shields. "Inspectors Kelstrom and Coretti. We're here about one of your tenants."

"That so? Which one?"

"The man's name is Feldstein, but I doubt he'd be using it."

"Feldstein?" The old man shook his head. "Nope, no one here by that name. Only a few of the rooms occupied now. We're closing up month after next. Building's being torn down."

"Is that right?"

"Yep. Don't know what I'm gonna do then. Retire, maybe, if I can find a place to live on my lousy pension." Noise erupted from the TV behind him. He cocked an ear, listened until the noise subsided. "I been watching the fights," he said. "Heavyweight match tonight. Not much of a scrap, though. They don't put on a show like they used to. You fellas fight fans?"

"No," I said. I wished I had some coffee, and to hell with what the doctor had said. It was damn cold in this rat trap. "These few tenants of yours. Any of them new, here just a couple of days?"

"Matter of fact, there is one fella. Day clerk didn't want to rent to him, on account of us closing up pretty soon, but he paid extra. Wish it'd been me on duty got that little bonus." He sighed. "Name's Collins. I only seen him once. Stays in his room, mostly."

"What does he look like?"

"Little guy, kind of skinny. Has a mole or something on his left cheek."

Coretti and I exchanged a glance. The description matched Feldstein's.

"He in his room now?" Coretti asked.

"Far as I know."

"What's his room number?"

"Three-o-six." The old man did some more peering. "There ain't going to be any trouble, is there?"

"Let's hope not," I said. "You just stay in your room and watch the rest of the fights."

"Sure. Sure thing, Inspector."

We left him and took the stairs up to the third floor. The hallway was lit only by a pale bulb on the wall at the far end. No sounds came from behind any of the closed doors we passed. When we reached 306, I stood against the wall on one side of the door and Coretti did the same on the other. Then I reached out and rapped sharply on the panel.

Inside, there was a faint creaking of bedsprings, then nothing but silence. I knocked again. Nothing. I felt the tiny hairs on my neck lift and my stomach started to ache. The cold, stale air seemed suddenly charged with tension.

We had our service revolvers drawn when a wary voice said from inside, "Who is it?"

"Night clerk," I said.

I thought it was a passable imitation of the old man's voice, but it wasn't. The slugs came fast, three of them, ripping jagged splinters from the wood and gouging plaster from the opposite wall. The reports seemed to echo for a couple of seconds. Then it was quiet again.

Coretti and I hugged the wall, waiting. After a little time I heard a faint scraping sound, another that I had no trouble identifying. Feldstein was trying to get out the window.

I stepped back to get leverage, moved over in front of the door and slammed my foot against the wood just above the knob. The lock ripped loose and the door banged against the inner wall. I went in low and to the left, Coretti right behind me. Feldstein was at the window, one leg over the sill, a pasteboard suitcase in one hand and a snubnosed revolver in the other. I threw myself to the floor as he fired, spoiling the shot I had at him. The bullet missed both of us. Coretti squeezed off in return, dodging, but he missed, too. In the next second Feldstein was out through the window and on the fire escape, a dim shadow in the rain.

I pulled up onto my knees, snapped a quick shot that shattered the window glass. Another miss. I heard the fugitive's heavy shoes pounding down the fire escape as I gained my feet. Coretti had gotten tangled up in a chair, I saw then. I yelled at him, "Downstairs, Bob! Cut him off in the alley!"

I ran to the window and got my head out. Not a smart move because Feldstein was directly below, with a clear upward slant. His first slug tore a hole in the window frame a few inches above my head, the second screamed off the railing in front of me and sprayed my face with iron filings.

Feldstein didn't wait to try a third shot. I could hear him running again. Cursing myself for a fool, the pain like a hot iron in my gut, I heaved myself through the window and crouched on the slats. He was at the second floor level now, scrambling down the rain-slick steps. I steadied my weapon and fired low, trying for his legs. That shot missed wide, but the next took him in the hip or thigh. I saw him buckle. He lost his grip on the suitcase and his arms flailed as he staggered sideways. He banged hard into the railing. The bar caught him just below the waist and pitched him over. I heard him scream once, just once, then the thud of his body slamming the alley floor below.

I straightened slowly, wiping sweat and rain off my face. Coretti was coming up the alley, running. I looked to see if anyone was behind him, roused by the gunfire, but there was no one.

The fire escape was one of the old-fashioned types that ended flush with the pavement. That made it easy for me to get down there in a hurry. Coretti was bent over Feldstein by then. I started toward him, and all of a sudden I couldn't seem to get any air into my lungs. A tongue of fire licked down from my stomach to my groin. I dropped to one knee, my head hanging down, fighting to breathe.

"Arne, you hit?" Coretti was beside me now, one hand on my shoulder.

"No. Ulcer . . . medicine . . ."

He found the bottle in my coat pocket, uncapped it, got some of the painkiller into me. It seemed to take a long time for it to work. When the hurt finally subsided and I could get my breath, he helped me to my feet.

"You okay now?"

"Better. Just give me a minute."

"Maybe I ought to call the paramedics . . ."

"No. I'm okay I tell you." The pain was almost completely gone. I sucked in some of the damp air, looking over to where Feldstein lay. "What about him?"

"Dead. Broken neck."

"We've got to radio in."

"Better get the suitcase first. Can you climb back up the stairs?"

I said I could, but I leaned on Coretti on the way up. I was pretty shaky, all right. At the second floor level, the pasteboard suitcase lay against the wire mesh of the railing. Coretti picked it up. When we reached the third floor and climbed back into Feldstein's room, I was oozing sweat.

Coretti laid the suitcase on the bed. I said, "Open it up, let's have a look." He nodded, flipped the catches, lifted the lid.

The suitcase was jammed full of money—fifties and hundreds in thick bundles. Plain wrappers with numbers written on them in pencil bound each stack. We stood there looking down at them, neither of us saying anything. The stench of cordite still lingered in the air.

I could feel tension rebuilding. Outside, the rain hammered in a steady cadence on the fire escape. The wind coming through the shattered window felt icy. In the hallway somebody coughed, somebody else said something in a low nervous voice. Other tenants. But they were hanging back, too scared to look in here. Coretti went over and yelled at them to get back in their rooms, then closed the door.

When he returned to the bed he said softly, "How much you think is in there, Arne?"

"I don't know."

Coretti began to take the bundles out of the suitcase, putting them on the bed. I didn't try to stop him. "If the numbers on those wrappers are right," he said when he was done, "there's a hundred and twelve thousand here. A hundred and twelve thousand dollars, Arne." His voice had a funny sound to it.

My throat was dry. I hadn't thought about the money before. A routine assignment, stolen cash, a thief in hiding—it happens every day, it's just a part of the job. But now, looking down at the bundles on the bed, the money took on weight, substance. It filled my thoughts. I kept staring at it, transfixed by it, more money than I would ever see again in my lifetime, and I was thinking what it would be like to have that much cash, half that much, enough to pay off the bulk of my debts, enough for the operation, enough so Gerry and I could start living decently.

It could be ours, it could be ours so damned easy. No one would ever know, we could tell them we didn't find any money here, it was dirty money anyway. It could be ours, one hundred and twelve thousand dollars, fifty-six thousand apiece . . .

My stomach throbbed again. I could hear my heart pounding. I was still sweating, sweating like a pig in this cold room.

"Arne?" Coretti's voice was almost a whisper.

I swallowed against the dryness in my throat. I didn't say anything.

"You're thinking it, too, aren't you."

"Yeah," I said, "I'm thinking it, too."

"We could do it, Arne."

"I don't know. Maybe, but . . . I don't know."

"We could do it," Coretti said again.

"In fifteen years I've never taken a penny. Never even fixed a parking ticket."

"Neither have I. But this isn't a piece of small-time graft, this is a hundred and twelve thousand dollars. A chance like this comes once in a lifetime. Just once."

"I know that, dammit."

He licked his lips. "Well?"

The windblown rain was coming down harder now. I could feel the chill wetness against my face. "It's a hell of a big risk. You know what'd happen if we got caught."

"Sure I know. But I say it's worth it. I say we won't get caught."

"If we claim there wasn't any money, the captain'll be suspicious."

"Let him be. What could he prove?"

"The day clerk probably saw the suitcase when Feldstein checked in."

"So we leave the suitcase. We can carry all the money in our pockets, under our coats."

"There'd still be an investigation."

"What could he *prove,* Arne?"

"As soon as we started spending the money they'd know."

"A little at a time," Coretti said. "That's what we do, parcel it out a little at a time. It's gambling money, there's no way the bills can be traced."

"Christ, Bob, you've been a cop as long as I have. It's the little things that trip you up, the unforeseen things. You know that as well as I do."

Coretti tongued his lips again.

"We'd go to prison," I said. "Think about your family. What becomes of them if that happens?"

"I am thinking about my family. I'm thinking about all the things I want my wife and kids to have that I can't give them. That's all I'm thinking about right now."

I kept looking at the money, and thinking, the way Coretti was, about the piled-up bills and the secondhand furniture and car and the second-rate clothing and all the doing without and the burning, throbbing thing that was eating a hole in the pit of my stomach. But at the same time I was thinking about the fifteen years I'd been a straight arrow, an honest cop, and the convictions a man has, the pattern of life he sets for himself, and what would happen if he were to sacrifice everything he believed in for one big gamble, one grab for the brass ring. Even if we got away with it, I knew that it would prey on my conscience, eat a hole in me bigger than the one in my gut and eventually destroy me.

I closed my eyes, and I saw Gerry's face, Gerry's proud smile, and I took a deep breath and opened my eyes and I said to Coretti, "No. I can't do it, I won't do it."

"Arne—"

"No, Bob. No."

Quickly, savagely, I began stuffing the bundles of cash back into the suitcase. Coretti grabbed my arm, but I shook it off and kept on refilling the case. When I was done I snapped the catch shut and hefted it and turned to face him.

"I'm going downstairs and report in," I said. "And I'm going to tell them about the money, every dollar of it. That's the way it's going to be, Bob. That's the way it *has* to be."

He didn't say anything. His eyes locked with mine.

"You going to try to stop me?" I said.

A few seconds passed before he said, "No," and stepped aside.

I went out into the hall and down the stairs, feeling the weight of the suitcase in my hand and against my leg, and I didn't look back. The old man was waiting in the lobby, his eyes big and scared behind his glasses. He rattled questions at me, but I shoved past him and went out to the sedan. I locked the suitcase in the trunk, then called the Hall and told them what had happened.

Afterward I sat waiting with the wheezing heater on high.

I'd been there five minutes when Coretti showed. He walked slowly to the passenger side and got in without looking at me. Both of us just sat there. The silence was as deep as it had been in the room upstairs.

He broke it by asking, "Did you report in?"

"Yeah."

Silence again. Then he said, "God help me, I almost shot you up there. When you were putting the money back in the suitcase. I almost pulled my weapon and shot you in the back."

I had nothing to say. What can you say to a thing like that?

"Don't you understand?" Coretti said. "I almost murdered you. You've been my friend and my partner for ten years and I almost blew you away."

"But you didn't," I said finally.

"But I almost did."

"Money like that . . . it can do funny things to a man. Think how we'd be, what we might do, if we'd taken it."

"Maybe you're right. I still think we could've gotten away with it. Now we'll never know. But it scared the hell out of me, what I almost did up there. I thought I knew myself, but now . . ." He shook his head.

"You think it was an easy decision for me, Bob?"

"I know it wasn't. Don't you think I know that?"

"The best thing for both of us is to try to forget it ever happened."

"I don't know if I can," Coretti said.

My hand wasn't steady as I reached into the pocket of my shirt for a cigarette. The pack was crushed and wet. I crumpled it, threw it into the back seat. Wordlessly Coretti extended his pack to me. I took one, and our eyes met again, briefly, then we both looked away.

I lit the cigarette and inhaled deeply, feeling the smoke

curl into my lungs. I stared out at the empty street and the falling rain, taking slow drags—and there was a savage tearing sensation under my breastbone, a fiery pain so intense I cried out. Then I couldn't breathe, couldn't move. My vision blurred. The last thing I saw was Coretti reaching out to me. And the last thing I heard was the high, keening wail of sirens slicing through the wet, black night.

I woke up in the hospital. Full of dope, hooked up to machines and an IV. I didn't feel any pain, but my middle was a mass of bandages. A nurse came in, looked at me, went away again. Then my doctor was there. He asked me how I was feeling. I told him groggy and then asked him, "What happened?"

"Exactly what I warned you might happen," he said. "Your ulcer perforated. You're a very lucky man, Mr. Kelstrom. You almost died on the operating table."

"Yeah," I said. "Lucky."

"If you'd listened to me when I first told you you needed an operation, this would not have happened. As it is . . . well, barring complications you should be all right in time."

"In time. What's that mean? How long am I going to be in here?"

"A few weeks. After that, two or three months convalescence at home."

"Weeks? Months?"

"Recovery from a perforated ulcer is a slow process, Mr. Kelstrom."

"I've got a wife and kid. How can I support my family if I'm flat on my back?"

"I'm sorry," the doctor said, "but you really have no one to blame but yourself."

He went away and the nurse came back and gave me some

more dope that knocked me out. When I woke up again, Gerry was there holding my hand.

"Oh, Arne," she said, "we almost lost you. Why didn't you tell me how bad the ulcer was? Why didn't you have the operation right away?"

"We couldn't afford it. All the damn bills . . ."

"We could've managed. We'll manage as it is, but—" She broke off and looked away. Then she put on a smile and said, "We'll be all right. Don't worry, everything's going to be fine."

I didn't say anything. This time I was the one who looked away.

Later, Coretti and the captain came in. They stood awkwardly, Coretti not making eye contact with me. The whole time he was there he looked at a spot on the wall above my head. The captain said some things about what a good cop I was, how he was putting Coretti and me up for departmental citations. He said I'd get full disability while I was recuperating. He said that if it turned out I couldn't work the field anymore, he'd see to it I had a desk job for as long as I wanted it. He didn't mention the money, but he didn't need to. We all knew that it would be unclaimed and eventually wind up going to the state.

Coretti didn't say a word until they were ready to leave. Then he said to the wall, "Good luck, Arne. Take care of yourself." That was all. After they were gone, I wondered if he'd be back to see me. I didn't think he would. I didn't think I'd be seeing much of him at all anymore.

I lay there and thought about the money. One hundred and twelve thousand dollars divided in two, fifty-six thousand dollars—the one big opportunity that I'd turned my back on. I thought about the fifteen years I'd been an honest, by-the-book cop, and all the bribes and payoffs, all the chances I'd had for some quick and easy cash that would have made my life and Gerry's life easier, all those other opportunities I'd let slip away because of convictions that you couldn't eat and couldn't pay the bills with.

We'll manage, Gerry had said. *Don't worry, everything's going to be fine.*

Well, I wasn't worrying. Not anymore. And everything *was* going to be fine. Because now I knew with a brand new conviction what I was going to do when I returned to duty.

I knew just exactly what I was going to do.

A Craving for Originality

Charlie Hackman was a professional writer. He wrote popular fiction, any kind from sexless Westerns to sexy Gothics to oversexed historical romances, whatever the current trends happened to be. He could be counted on to deliver an acceptable manuscript to order in two weeks. He had published 9,000,000 words in a fifteen-year career, under a variety of different names (Allison St. Cyr being the most prominent), and he couldn't tell you the plot of any book he'd written more than six months ago. He was what is euphemistically known in the trade as "a dependable wordsmith," or "a versatile pro," or "a steady producer of commercial commodities."

In other words, he was well-named: Hackman was a hack.

The reason he was a hack was not because he was fast and prolific, or because he contrived popular fiction on demand, or because he wrote for money. It was because he was and did all these things with no ambition and no sense of commitment. It was because he wrote without originality of any kind.

Of course, Hackman had not started out to be a hack; no writer does. But he had discovered early on, after his first two novels were rejected with printed slips by thirty-seven publishers each, that (a) he was not very good, and (b) what talent he did possess was in the form of imitations. When he tried to do imaginative, ironic, meaningful work of his own he failed miserably; but when he imitated the ideas and visions of others, the blurred carbon copies he produced were just literate enough to be publishable.

Truth to tell, this didn't bother him very much. The one thing he had always wanted to be was a professional writer; he had dreamed of nothing else since his discovery of the Hardy Boys and Tarzan books in his pre-teens. So from the time of his first sale he accepted what he was, shrugged, and told himself not to worry about it. What was wrong with being a hack, anyway? The writing business was full of them—and hacks, no less than nonhacks, offered a desirable form of escapist entertainment to the masses; the only difference was, his readership had nondiscriminating tastes. Was his product, after all, any less honorable than what television offered? Was he hurting anybody, corrupting anybody? No. Absolutely not. So what was wrong with being a hack?

For one and a half decades, operating under this cheerful set of rationalizations, Hackman was a complacent man. He wrote from ten to fifteen novels per year, all for minor and exploitative paperback houses, and earned an average annual sum of $35,000. He married an ungraceful woman named Grace and moved into a suburban house on Long Island. He went bowling once a week, played poker once a week, argued conjugal matters with his wife once a week, and took the train into Manhattan to see his agent and editors once a week. Every June he and Grace spent fourteen pleasant days at Lake George in the Adirondacks. Every Christmas Grace's mother came from Pennsylvania and spent fourteen miserable days with them.

He drank a little too much sometimes and worried about lung cancer because he smoked three packs of cigarettes a day. He cheated moderately on his income tax. He coveted one of his neighbors' wives. He read all the current paperback bestsellers, dissected them in his mind, and then reassembled them into similar plots for his own novels. When new acquaintances asked him what he did for a living he said, "I'm a writer," and seldom failed to feel a small glow of pride.

That was the way it was for fifteen years—right up until the morning of his fortieth birthday.

Hackman woke up on that morning, looked at Grace lying beside him, and realized she had put on at least forty pounds since their marriage. He listened to himself wheeze as he lit his first cigarette of the day. He got dressed and walked downstairs to his office, where he read the half page of manuscript still in his typewriter (an occult pirate novel, the latest craze). He went outside and stood on the lawn and looked at his house. Then he sat down on the porch steps and looked at himself.

I'm not just a writer of hack stories, he thought sadly, I'm a liver of a hack life.

Fifteen years of cohabiting with trite fictional characters in hackneyed fictional situations. Fifteen years of cohabiting with an unimaginative wife in a trite suburb in a hackneyed lifestyle in a conventional world. Hackman the hack, doing the same things over and over again; Hackman the hack, grinding out books and days one by one. No uniqueness in any of it, from the typewriter to the bedroom to the Adirondacks.

No originality.

He sat there for a long while, thinking about this. No originality. Funny. It was like waking up to the fact that, after forty years, you've never tasted pineapple, that pineapple was missing from your life. All of a sudden you craved pineapple; you wanted it more than you'd ever wanted anything before. Pineapple or originality—it was the same principle.

Grace came out eventually and asked him what he was doing. "Thinking that I crave originality," he said, and she said, "Will you settle for eggs and bacon?" Trite dialogue, Hackman thought. Hackneyed humor. He told her he didn't want any breakfast and went into his office.

Originality. Well, even a hack ought to be able to create something fresh and imaginative if he applied himself; even a hack learned a few tricks in fifteen years. How about a short story? Good. He had never written a short story, he would be working in new territory already. Now how about a plot?

He sat at his typewriter. He paced the office. He lay down on the couch. He sat at the typewriter again. Finally the germ of an idea came to him and he nurtured it until it began to develop. Then he began to type.

It took him all day to write the story, which was about five thousand words long. That was his average wordage per day on a novel, but on a novel he never revised so much as a comma. After supper he went back into the office and made pen-and-ink corrections until eleven o'clock. Then he went to bed, declined Grace's reluctant offer of "a birthday present," and dreamed about the story until 6:00 A.M. At which time he got up, retyped the pages, made some more revisions in ink, and retyped the story a third time before he was satisfied. He mailed it that night to his agent.

Three days later the agent called about a new book contract. Hackman asked him, "Did you have a chance to read the short story I sent you?"

"I read it, all right. And sent it straight back to you."

"Sent it back? What's wrong with it?"

"It's old hat," the agent said. "The idea's been done to death."

Hackman went out into the backyard and lay down in the hammock. All right, so maybe he was doomed to hackdom as a writer; maybe he just wasn't capable of *writing* anything original. But that didn't mean he couldn't *do* something original, did it? He had a quick mind, a good grasp of what was going on in the world. He ought to be able to come up with at least one original idea, maybe even an idea that would not only satisfy his craving for originality but change his life, get him out of the stale rut he was in.

He closed his eyes.

He concentrated.

He thought about jogging backward from Long Island to Miami Beach and then applying for an entry in the Guinness Book of World Records.

Imitative.

He thought about marching naked through Times Square at high noon, waving a standard paperback contract and using a bullhorn to protest man's literary inhumanity to man.

Trite.

He thought about adopting a red-white-and-blue disguise and robbing a bank in each one of the original thirteen states.

Derivative.

He thought about changing his name to Holmes, finding a partner named Watson, and opening a private inquiry agency that specialized in solving the unsolved and insoluble.

Parrotry.

He thought about doing other things legal and illegal, clever and foolish, dangerous and harmless.

Unoriginal. Unoriginal. Unoriginal.

That day passed and several more just like it. Hackman became obsessed with originality—so much so that he found himself unable to write, the first serious block he had had as a professional. It was maddening, but every time he thought of a sentence and started to type it out, something would click in his mind and make him analyze it as original or banal. The verdict was always banal.

He thought about buying a small printing press, manufacturing bogus German Deutsche marks in his basement, and then flying to Munich and passing them at the Oktoberfest.

Counterfeit.

Hackman took to drinking a good deal more than his usual allotment of alcohol in the evenings. His consumption of cigarettes rose to four packs a day and climbing. His originality quotient remained at zero.

He thought about having a treasure map tattooed on his chest, claiming to be the sole survivor of a gang of armored car thieves, and conning all sorts of greedy people out of their life savings.

Trite.

The passing days turned into passing weeks. Hackman still wasn't able to write; he wasn't able to do much of anything except vainly overwork his brain cells. He knew he couldn't function again as a writer or a human being until he did something, *anything* original.

He thought about building a distillery in his garage and becoming Long Island's largest manufacturer and distributor of bootleg whiskey.

Hackneyed.

Grace had begun a daily and voluble series of complaints. Why was he moping around, drinking and smoking so much? Why didn't he go into his office and write his latest piece of trash? What were they going to do for money if he didn't fulfill his contracts? How would they pay the mortgage and the rest of their bills? What was the *matter* with him, anyway? Was he going through some kind of midlife crisis or what?

Hackman thought about strangling her, burying her body under the acacia tree in the backyard—committing the perfect crime.

Stale. Bewhiskered.

Another week disappeared. Hackman was six weeks

overdue now on an occult pirate novel and two weeks overdue on a male-action novel; his publishers were upset, his agent was upset; where the hell were the manuscripts? Hackman said he was just polishing up the first one. "Sure you are," the agent said over the phone. "Well, you'd better have it with you when you come in on Friday. I mean that, Charlie. You'd better deliver."

Hackman thought about kidnapping the star of Broadway's top musical extravaganza and holding her for a ransom of $1,000,000 plus a role in her next production.

Old stuff.

He decided that things couldn't go on this way. Unless he came up with an original idea pretty soon, he might just as well shuffle off this mortal coil.

He thought about buying some rat poison and mixing himself an arsenic cocktail.

More old stuff.

Or climbing a utility pole and grabbing hold of a high-tension wire.

Prosaic. Corny.

Or hiring a private plane to fly him over the New Jersey swamps and then jumping out at two thousand feet.

Ho-hum.

Damn! He couldn't seem to go on, he couldn't seem not to go on. So what was he going to do?

He thought about driving over to Pennsylvania, planting certain carefully faked documents inside Grace's mother's house, and turning the old bat in to the F.B.I. as a foreign spy.

Commonplace.

On Friday morning he took his cigarettes (the second of the five packs a day he was now consuming) and his latest hangover down to the train station. There he boarded the express for Manhattan and took a seat in the club car.

He thought about hijacking the train and extorting $20,000,000 from the state of New York.

Imitative.

When the train arrived in Manhattan he trudged the six blocks to his agent's office. In the elevator on the way up an attractive young blonde gave him a friendly smile and said it was a nice day, wasn't it?

Hackman thought about making her his mistress, having a torrid affair, and then running off to Acapulco with her and living in sin in a villa high above the harbor and weaving Mexican serapes by day and drinking tequila by night.

Hackneyed.

The first thing his agent said to him was, "Where's the manuscript, Charlie?" Hackman said it wasn't ready yet, he was having a few personal problems. The agent said, "You think you got problems? What about my problems? You think I can afford to have hack writers missing deadlines and making editors unhappy? That kind of stuff reflects back on me, ruins my reputation. I'm not in this business for my health, so maybe you'd better just find yourself another agent."

Hackman thought about bashing him over the head with a paperweight, disposing of the body, and assuming his identity after first gaining sixty pounds and going through extensive plastic surgery.

Moth-eaten. Threadbare.

Out on the street again, he decided he needed a drink and turned into the first bar he came to. He ordered a triple vodka and sat brooding over it. I've come to the end of my rope, he thought. If there's one original idea in this world, I can't even imagine what it is. For that matter, I can't even imagine a partly original idea, which I'd settle for right now because maybe there isn't anything completely original any more.

"What am I going to do?" he asked the bartender.

"Who cares?" the bartender said. "Stay, go, drink, don't drink—it's all the same to me."

Hackman sighed and got off his stool and swayed out onto East 52nd Street. He turned west and began to walk back toward Grand Central, jostling his way through the mid-afternoon crowds. Overhead, the sun glared down at him between the buildings like a malevolent eye.

He was nearing Madison Avenue, muttering clichés to himself, when the idea struck him.

It came out of nowhere, full-born in an instant, the way most great ideas (or so he had heard) always do. He came to an abrupt standstill. Then he began to smile. Then he began to laugh. Passersby gave him odd looks and detoured around him, but Hackman didn't care. The idea was all that mattered.

It was inspired.

It was imaginative.

It was meaningful.

It was original.

Oh, not one-hundred-percent original—but that was all right. He had already decided that finding total originality was an impossible goal. This idea was close, though. It was close and it was wonderful and he was going to do it. Of course he was going to do it; after all these weeks of search and frustration, how could he not do it?

Hackman set out walking again. His stride was almost jaunty and he was whistling to himself. Two blocks south he entered a sporting goods store and found what he wanted. The salesman who waited on him asked if he was going camping. "Nope," Hackman said, and winked. "Something *much* more original than that."

He left the store and hurried down to Madison to a bookshop that specialized in mass-market paperbacks. Inside were several long rows of shelving, each shelf containing different categories of fiction and nonfiction, alphabetically arranged. Hackman stepped into the fiction section, stopped in front of the shelf marked "Historical Romances," and squinted at the titles until he located one of his own pseudonymous works. Then he unwrapped his parcel.

And took out the woodsman's hatchet.

And got a comfortable grip on its handle.

And raised it high over his head.

And—

Whack! Eleven copies of *Love's Tender Fury* by Allison St. Cyr were drawn and quartered.

A male customer yelped; a female customer shrieked. Hackman took no notice. He moved on to the shelf marked "Occult Pirate Adventure," raised the hatchet again, and—

Whack! Nine copies of *The Devil Daughter of Jean Lafitte* by Adam Caine were exorcised and scuttled.

On to "Adult Westerns." And—

Whack! Four copies of *Lust Rides the Outlaw Trail* by Galen McGee bit the dust.

Behind the front counter a chubby little man was jumping up and down, waving his arms. "What are you doing?" he kept shouting at Hackman. "What are you doing?"

"Hackwork!" Hackman shouted back. "I'm a hack writer doing hackwork!"

He stepped smartly to "Gothic Suspense." And—

Whack! Five copies of *Mansion of Dread* by Melissa Ann Farnsworth were reduced to rubble.

On to "Male Action Series," and—

Whack! Ten copies of Max Ruffe's *The Grenade Launcher #23: Blowup at City Hall* exploded into fragments.

Hackman paused to survey the carnage. Then he nodded in satisfaction and turned toward the front door. The bookshop was empty now, but the chubby little man was visible on the sidewalk outside, jumping up and down and semaphoring his arms amid a gathering crowd. Hackman crossed to the door in purposeful strides and threw it open.

People scattered every which way when they saw him come out with the hatchet aloft. But they needn't have feared; he had no interest in people, except as bit players in this little drama. After all, what hack worth the name ever cared a hoot about his audience?

He began to run up 48th Street toward Fifth Avenue, brandishing the hatchet. Nobody tried to stop him, not even when he lopped off the umbrella shading a frankfurter vendor's cart.

"I'm a hack!" he shouted.

And shattered the display window of an exclusive boutique.

"I'm Hackman the hack!" he yelled.

And halved the product and profits of a pretzel vendor.

"I'm Hackman the hack and I'm hacking my way to glory!" he bellowed.

And sliced the antenna off an illegally parked Cadillac limousine.

He was almost to Fifth Avenue by this time. Ahead of him he could see a red signal light holding up crosstown traffic; this block of 48th Street was momentarily empty. Behind him he could hear angry shouts and what sounded like a police whistle. He looked back over his shoulder. Several people were giving pursuit, including the chubby little man from the bookshop; the leader of the pack, a blue uniform with a red face atop it, was less than fifty yards distant.

But the game was not up yet, Hackman thought. There

were more bookstores along Fifth; with any luck he could hack his way through two or three before they got him. He decided south was the direction he wanted to go, pulled his head around, and started to sprint across the empty expanse of 48th.

Only the street wasn't empty any longer; the signal on Fifth had changed to green for the eastbound traffic.

He ran right out in front of an oncoming car.

He saw it too late to jump clear, and the driver saw him too late to brake or swerve. But before he and the machine joined forces, Hackman had just enough time to realize the full scope of what was happening—and to feel a sudden elation. In fact, he wished with his last wish that he'd thought of this himself. It was the crowning touch, the final fillip, the *coup de grace;* it lent the death of Hackman, unlike the life of Hackman, a genuine originality.

Because the car that did him in was not just a car; it was a New York City taxi cab.

Otherwise known as a hack.

One of Those Cases

A "Nameless Detective" Story

It was one of those cases you take on when you're on your uppers. You want to turn it down—it's an old story, a sordid one, a sad one—but you know you can't afford to. So you look into tear-filmed eyes, and you sigh, and you say yes . . .

Her name was Judith Paige. She was in her late twenties, attractive in a quiet, shy sort of way. She had pale blonde hair, china-blue eyes, and the kind of translucent white skin that seems brittle and makes you think of opaque and finely blown glass. Until the previous year, she had lived in a small town in Idaho and had come to San Francisco "to search for some meaning in life." Which probably meant that she had come looking for a husband.

And she'd found one, a salesman named Walter Paige. They had been married six weeks now, and it was something less than the idyllic union she had expected. It wasn't that Paige abused her in any way, or was a drinker or a gambler; it was just that, in the past month, he'd taken to leaving her alone in the evenings. He told her it was business—he worked for a real estate firm out near the Cow Palace—and when she pressed him for details he grew short-tempered. He was working on a couple of large prospects, he said, that would set them up for the future.

She figured he was working on another woman.

Like I said: an old, sordid, sad story. And one of those cases.

She wanted me to follow him for a few days, either to confirm or deny her suspicions. That was all. You don't need to prove adultery, or much of anything else, to obtain a divorce in the state of California these days, so I would not be required to testify in any civil proceedings. It was just that she had to know, one way or the other—the tears starting then—and if she were right, she wanted to dissolve the marriage and go back to Idaho. She had a little money saved and could pay my standard rates; and she was sure I was honest and capable, which meant that she hoped I wouldn't take advantage of her in any way.

I sat there behind my desk feeling old and tired and cynical. It was a nice day outside, and I had the window open a little; the breeze off the Bay was cool and fresh, but the air I was pulling into my lungs tasted sour somehow. I lit a cigarette. And then took one of the contract forms out of the bottom drawer and slid it over for her to examine.

When she had, without much interest, I drew it back and filled it out and had her sign it. Then I said, "All right, Mrs. Paige. What time does your husband come home from work?"

"Usually about six o'clock."

"Does he use public transportation or drive?"

"He drives."

"What kind of car?"

"A dark blue VW."

"License number?"

"It has one of those personalized plates. WALLY P."

"Uh-huh. What time does he leave again when he goes out?"

"Right after supper," Mrs. Paige said. "Seven-thirty or so."

"He comes back at what time?"

"Around midnight."

"How often does this happen?"

"Four or five times a week, lately."

"Any particular nights?"

"No, not really."

"Saturdays and Sundays?"

"Saturdays, sometimes. Not Sundays, though. He . . . he always spends that day with me."

Never on Sunday, I thought sourly. I said, "Which real estate company does he work for?"

"I'm sorry," she said, "I don't know. Walter is very closemouthed about his job."

"He's never told you where he works?"

"Well, he did once, but I can't remember it. Is it important?"

"Probably not." I put down the pencil I had been using to take notes. "I think I have everything I need for now, Mrs. Paige. I'll be on the job tonight if your husband goes out."

"You won't let him know you're following him, will you? I mean, if I'm wrong and he's, well, just working, I wouldn't want him to know what I've done."

"I'll be as careful as I can."

"Thank you," she said, and dabbed at her eyes with her handkerchief and cleared her throat. "Will you call me as soon as you find out anything?"

"Right away."

"I'll give you a check. Will fifty dollars be all right?"

"Fine."

I looked away while she made out the check, out through the window. Sunlight and bright blue sky softened the look of the ugly, crumbling buildings in the Tenderloin. Even the panhandlers and dope pushers seemed to be enjoying the weather; they were out in droves this afternoon.

A nice day for a lot of people, all right. But not for Judith Paige and not for me.

At seven o'clock I was sitting behind the wheel of my car, parked four buildings down and on the opposite side of the street from the stucco-fronted apartment house the Paiges lived in. The dark blue VW with the WALLY P license plates was thirty feet away, facing in the same direction.

This was a fairly well-to-do neighborhood in the Parkside district; kids were out playing, husbands and wives were still arriving home from work. If you're staked out in an area like that, you run a risk by sitting around in a parked car for any length of time. People get suspicious, and the next thing you know, you've got a couple of patrol cops pulling up and asking questions. But if you don't stay more than an hour, and if you keep glancing at your watch and show signs of increasing annoyance, you can get away with it; the residents tend to think you're waiting for somebody and leave you alone. I expected to be here less than an hour, so I wasn't worried.

I went through the watch-checking-and-annoyance routine, smoked a couple of cigarettes and glanced through a 1949 issue of *FBI Detective* that I'd brought along to help pass the time. And at twenty of eight, Paige came out and walked straight to the VW. The sun had gone down by then, but there was still enough reddish twilight to let me see that he was a tall, slender guy dressed in a blue suit, with one of those toothbrush mustaches that looked from a distance like a caterpillar humped on his upper lip.

I started my car just as he swung out, and I let him have a half-block lead before I went after him. He drove without hurry, observing the speed limits. Whenever possible, I put another car between us—and on the four-lane streets like

Ocean Avenue, I used the lane opposite to the one he was in. You pick up ways and means like that over the years, but if you're following a pro, or somebody alert to the possibility of a tail, there's not much you can do; the subject will spot you nine times out of ten.

Paige was not expecting a tail, though, and I had no trouble staying with him. We picked up Highway 280 near the City College, followed it to where it connects with the Bayshore Freeway southbound. Fifteen minutes later, Paige exited in South San Francisco and went up Grand Avenue and finally turned into the parking lot of a big shopping center. He parked near a large cut-rate liquor store. I put my car into a slot in the next row, watched him get out and enter the liquor store. Five minutes later, he came back out with a bottle of some kind in a small paper sack and got back into his car. But he didn't go anywhere—he just sat there.

I figured it this way: Paige was playing around, all right, and the woman he was playing with was probably married as well, which necessitated a neutral meeting ground. He was waiting for her now, and when she arrived they would go to a motel or maybe to a little love nest they had set up somewhere—and that would be it as far as I was concerned. I'd get the license number of the woman's car when she showed, then follow her and Paige to wherever it was they had their assignations. Then I would call Mrs. Paige and listen to her cry; they always cry when you tell them, even though they expect the worst. And then I would go home and try to sleep.

So we sat there in the lot, Paige and I, waiting. It got to be nine o'clock; most of the stores were closing for the night, and there were not nearly as many cars as there had been earlier. I thought that if the lot became too empty, I would have to move out to the street somewhere; I did not want

Paige noticing me, questioning the presence of another guy waiting alone as he was doing.

At nine-thirty, the woman still hadn't shown up. Everything was closed in the center except the liquor store and a bowling alley over at the far end. I had about decided it was time for me to move when Paige abruptly got out of the VW and headed toward the bowling alley.

He's going to call her, I thought. He wants to know why she stood him up tonight.

I let him get inside the building before I followed. League bowlers were occupying all twenty lanes in there; after the relative silence of the past hour, the noise was deafening. I went down by the coffee shop, where there was a phone booth, but I didn't see Paige anywhere. I came back and went into the bar. He was there, in another booth, talking animatedly on the phone.

I found a place to sit at the bar where I could see the booth in the back-bar mirror and ordered a beer. It was close to ten minutes before Paige finished his conversation. He stopped at the bar long enough to toss off a shot of bourbon neat; he did not even glance in my direction. I gave him two minutes and then moved after him.

He was just pulling out of the lot when I reached my car. I got going in plenty of time to pick him up, but it was pointless, really: he led me straight back to San Francisco and the Parkside district. From down the block, with my headlights dark, I watched him park the VW and then enter his apartment building. He didn't come out again in the next ten minutes.

I said to hell with it and went home to bed.

In the morning, from my office, I called Judith Paige and made my report. She tried to muffle her tears, but I could hear the sob in her voice; it grated at my nerves like fingernails across a blackboard.

"Then . . . then it's true, isn't it?" she said. "Walter has another woman."

"I'll be blunt with you, Mrs. Paige," I said, even though I did not feel blunt at all. "The chances of it are pretty good. He wasn't working last night, and he was obviously waiting for someone in that parking lot."

"But there's still a chance that he was there for some other reason, isn't there?"

"Yes, there's a chance."

"I have to be sure," she said. "You understand, don't you?"

"I understand."

"You'll be here tonight?"

"Yes, Mrs. Paige," I said. "I'll be there."

Paige did not leave that night until after eight.

I was beginning to think that he wasn't going at all, and I was growing nervous about sitting there much longer, when he finally appeared. He got into the VW and led me along the same route he had last night, past the City College and onto 280. I decided he was heading for the same shopping center in South San Francisco; I dropped back a little, giving him plenty of room. And that was just where he went.

He parked in about the same place. I took a slot farther back this time and a little more to one side, in the event we were in for another long wait past the closing time of the center's shops.

It developed just that way. Nine-thirty came, and then ten, and the parking area was just about empty. But it was dark where I was, and I had slumped low in the seat with the window down and my eyes on a level with the sill. I was pretty sure Paige couldn't see me from where he was.

So we waited, and I was about ready to call it another bust. Damn it, I thought, why doesn't she come? This kind of job played on my nerves anyway; the waiting only made it worse. If she was—

There was movement at the periphery of my vision. When I turned my head, I saw a lone figure hurrying across the darkened lot from the direction of the bowling alley. It moved in a straight line toward Paige's car, glancing left and right, its gaze flicking over my car but not lingering. And when it got to the VW and opened the door and slipped inside, the flash of the dome light let me see a leather jacket, jeans—crew-cut hair.

Paige's visitor was a man, not a woman.

What the hell? I thought. Paige had not struck me as the homosexual type, but then you never knew these days who might have leanings in that direction; I could not figure any other immediate explanation for this kind of meeting. I sat there thinking about Mrs. Paige, waiting for them to leave.

Only they didn't leave, not yet. The driver's door opened and Paige stepped out; he was wearing a hat now, a long overcoat that he must have put on while he'd been sitting in the darkness. Dimly, I could see the other guy slide over under the wheel. Paige walked to the liquor store, went inside. There was no other activity at this end of the lot—and no one else had entered the liquor store in the past five minutes.

I began to get it then, but by the time I put it all together it was too late for me to do anything about it. The new guy started the VW and took it slowly toward the lot's entrance a few doors down from the liquor store, keeping it clear of the bright outspill from the store's fluorescent lighting. I couldn't see what was happening inside the store, because of the angle.

Three minutes after he'd gone inside, Paige came running

out with one hand jammed up under his coat and the other gripping a small sack of some kind. He ran down to where the other guy had the VW rolling forward, jerked open the door and jumped in. The car pitched ahead, burning a little rubber, and when it turned east out of the lot its headlights came on for the first time. There was no movement over at the liquor store, no one in the lot to see or wonder what had happened except me.

I'd had the engine of my car going before Paige appeared, but I stayed where I was until the VW was a half-block away. Then I went after it, running dark, hanging back as far as I could without losing sight of its taillights.

The other car was moving fast but not recklessly; they must have figured they'd pulled it off clean, and they didn't want to call attention to themselves. The streets were dark here, except for intermittent house lights and the yellow puddles cast by street lamps. Clouds had begun to pile up, blotting out the moon: that made it all the darker and easier for me to follow without being seen. I was able to stay within a block of them.

They were heading for Hillside Boulevard; I could tell that before we'd gone a dozen blocks. That road runs along the western foot of the San Bruno Mountains, connecting to the southeast with the Bayshore Freeway and to the northeast with Daly City. It was a toss-up as to which way they would turn when they got there.

I wasn't at all sure now that I was doing the right thing. Maybe I should have gone into the liquor store to check on the clerk, make sure he was all right; then I could have telephoned the local police and given them Paige's name and that WALLY P license plate of his. But my instinctive reaction had been to give chase, to be able to pinpoint them when I finally did make the call. Wise or not, I had made my choice and I would have to stand by it.

When the VW neared Hillside Boulevard, I dropped back to see how it would go. They turned left. Daly City, then, and on into San Francisco that way. Or maybe they had another destination along the line.

I could still see the red glow of their taillights when I got to the intersection, but they were diminishing rapidly: the driver had opened it up now. It would have been too dangerous for me to try driving that dark road without lights; I switched on my headlamps before I made the turn. And then bore down on the accelerator to match their speed.

As I drove, I thought about how wrong Mrs. Paige and I had been about her husband. He didn't have another woman, or if he did she had nothing to do with these nocturnal outings of his. They were all explainable in the same way. There had been a string of liquor store holdups the past month, in a different Bay Area city each time—two men, one to pull the job and the other to drive the car. I hadn't thought of Paige in connection with the holdups; there was no reason I should have. I had been hired to investigate infidelity, not armed robbery.

So Paige and this other guy were the heisters; and that put an altogether different explanation on last night's events. Paige hadn't been waiting at the shopping center for anyone; he'd been casing the liquor store—the same thing he had probably done the past few nights, and on some or all of the other jobs they'd pulled. He would have been checking on how much traffic went in and out of the lot around this time of night, how many clerks and customers there were in the store, things like that. When he'd gone to the bowling alley, it had been to call his partner and make a report. It had looked good to them, and they were ready, and so they'd set it up for tonight.

The only things that weren't clear were why the other guy had showed up at the parking lot on foot instead of meeting Paige and driving there with him, and why they were using Paige's VW, with that easy-to-remember WALLY P license plate, as the getaway car. But I could find out the answers to those questions later on. They didn't matter much at this point.

What mattered was staying with those two, seeing to it they were arrested and put away. What mattered was how Judith Paige would feel when she found out her husband was something much worse than unfaithful . . .

The VW was in Colma now, a small community that had the dubious distinction of being the primary burial grounds for the San Francisco area. There were a dozen different cemeteries along here, and one golf course—Cypress Hills—sitting there incongruously in the middle of it all. This stretch of Hillside Boulevard was very dark; no other cars moved on it in either direction.

Another tenth of a mile clicked off on my odometer. And then the VW's brake lights came on ahead, and the car made a sharp right-hand turn into Cynthia Street—a narrow lane that marked the boundary between the golf course on the right and Mount Olivet Cemetery on the left. At its upper end, there were a couple of short dead-end streets and the looming black shapes of the San Bruno Mountains. Maybe the one guy lived there, I thought, and they were going to his place. Or maybe they were planning to stop for a few minutes and split the take from the liquor store.

I slowed, waiting until the VW passed behind a screen of eucalyptus lining the lane, then switched off my lights and swung up after them. The other car was better than a hundred yards ahead by then. We traveled a fifth of a mile with that much distance between us—and suddenly the taillights winked out, their headlights did the same and heavy darkness folded in on the road.

I punched the brake pedal, thinking they'd pull off onto the shoulder, getting ready to do the same thing. Only then the VW's backup lights flared, and when I heard the sharp whine of its engine in reverse I realized what a damned fool I'd been. They knew I was there, they had known it all along; somehow they'd spotted me tailing them. So they'd maneuvered me up here, where it was isolated, with the idea of ramming me, forcing me off the road.

I said a short, vicious word and managed to do three things at once: jammed the gearshift lever into reverse with my right hand, found the headlight switch and flicked it on with my left hand, and brought my left foot down on the high-beam button on the floor. The car leaped backward, yawing a little. The VW was almost on top of me by then, a hurtling black-and-red shape; its rear end missed my front bumper by a foot or less, then veered off toward the fence bordering the cemetery on the left. The guy behind the wheel had to fight it around, straighten out again, and that gave me a couple of extra seconds.

Hunched around on the seat now, I leaned over the back to look through the rear window and pushed the accelerator all the way down. The high white glare of my headlights, the crimson wash from my backup lights, bleached the darkness enough so that I could see the road behind me. It was pretty straight, and I had a white-fisted grip on the wheel. I kept my eyes on the road, not looking to see where the VW was; the metallic taste of fear was sharp in my mouth. I wasn't armed—I had not carried a gun since I'd been on the cops years ago—and these characters had at least one and probably two weapons. I had nowhere to go if I lost control of the car or they managed to get me off the road.

The intersection with Hillside Boulevard came up quickly, less than a hundred yards away now. Sweat half-blinded me, but when I dropped below the screen of trees I could see there were headlights approaching from the direction of South San Francisco—two sets of them. Relief dulled the edge of my fear. The nearest set of lights was maybe five hundred yards off: enough time, just enough time.

There was a sudden, glancing impact: the VW had rammed me, but not hard enough to do the job for them. I managed to keep the rear end straight as the intersection rushed up, held off using the brakes as long as I could; then I touched them lightly and laid my other hand on the horn ring and swung the wheel hard to the right. The tires screamed as I slid sideways, rocking, out onto Hillside Boulevard.

Another horn blared; there was more shrieking of rubber. The first of the oncoming cars swerved to the left, nosing off the road, to avoid a collision with me; the second braked hard and skidded around to the side of the first one—and in the next second a red light began revolving on its roof, sweeping the darkness with an eerie pulsing glow. It was a county police cruiser, a traffic unit that patrols Hillside for speeders at night.

I turned my head to see where the VW was, saw it right in front of me. They had swung out in the same direction I had, but the red light on the cruiser had made them quit worrying about me. The little car rocked as the transmission was thrown into a forward gear; rubber howled again. They had been half turned around on the road, as I had been, and they tried to come out of it too fast, with too much power. The rear end fishtailed and they started to slide one way, then the other. And then the VW spun around twice in the middle of the road, like a toy car in the hands of a playful kid; tilted and went over, rolling; finally settled on its top in the culvert between the road and the cemetery fence.

The county patrol car slid around mine and cut diagonally in front, blocking me off. One of the two cops who came out of it ran to where the VW lay in the culvert like a huge beetle on its back, wheels spinning lazily in the light-spattered darkness; the other cop came over to me with his service revolver drawn. He looked in through the open window. "What the hell's going on here?" he demanded.

I told him—as much as he needed to know right away. It took him a couple of minutes to believe me, but when I showed him the photostat of my investigator's license and told him what he would find in the wreckage, he was convinced. He left me to use his car radio, because the other cop was still at the wrecked VW and yelling for an ambulance and a tow truck; Paige and his partner were wedged inside, and he couldn't tell if they were dead or alive.

I was pretty shaky for a while, but by the time the ambulance and the tow truck arrived I was all right. A couple of guys went to work on the VW with blowtorches. When they got Paige and the other one out, they were still alive but cut up and unconscious; Paige had a broken leg, too. The ambulance took them away to the nearest emergency hospital.

The county officers escorted me to the police station in South San Francisco, where I made a formal statement. None of the cops was too pleased that I had given chase after the robbery, instead of notifying the law like a good citizen was supposed to do, but they didn't make an issue of it. They let me go on home after a couple of hours.

I had bad dreams that night. But they could not have been any worse than the dreams Judith Paige would be having.

In the morning I learned that Paige was an ex-con—four years at San Quentin for armed robbery—who'd figured that his job as a real estate salesman wasn't paying off and wasn't likely to. Two months ago, he'd reestablished contact with another armed robber he'd met in prison, and they had worked out the liquor store heists. The other guy's name was Stryker.

The rest was about as I'd figured it. Stryker, alert and strung out after the holdup, had spotted me coming out of the lot after them. They'd figured me for a heroic-citizen type, and at first they'd thought of trying to outrun me; but the VW didn't have all that much power, they had no idea how good a driver I was and they didn't want to risk alerting a cop by exceeding the speed limits. So they'd hit on Cynthia Street—and although they refused to admit it to the police, they would have killed me if they'd succeeded in forcing me off the road.

As for why Stryker had been on foot that night—and why they'd used Paige's VW, with its distinctive WALLY P license plate, instead of Stryker's car—the reason was so simple and ironic that it made me laugh sardonically when I heard it. Stryker lived down the Peninsula, near South San Francisco, and he was married, and his wife had insisted on using their car to attend an audition: she was a singer, and there was a job she badly wanted in the city. So he'd given in, notified Paige and then had her drop him off at the shopping center on her way into San Francisco.

Crooks, I thought. Christ!

There was irony, too, in the fact that Paige had apparently been faithful to Judith all along. He had married her because he loved her, or had some feeling for her. If she hadn't suspected him of playing around, and come to me, he and Stryker might have carried on their string of liquor store heists for quite a while before they screwed up and got themselves caught.

The police had been the ones to break the news to Judith Paige last night; better them than me. But I knew I had to see her again anyway: it was one of those things you have to do. So I drove out to the Parkside district late that afternoon and spent twenty minutes with her—twenty long minutes that were not easy for either of us.

She told me she was going to file for divorce and then go home to Idaho, which struck me as the wisest decision she could have made. She would meet another guy there someday, and she'd get remarried, and maybe then she would be happy. I hoped so.

I would never see her again in any case, but the future would still bring me another Judith Paige. There is always another Judith Paige for somebody in my business. One of these days she would walk into my office, and I would hear the old story again—the old, sad, sordid story.

Only that next time it would probably be true.

I Didn't Do It

Well, I keep telling you I didn't do it. I don't care how much evidence there is. You got to believe me. I didn't do it.

Sure, I was out there that night. I already admitted that, didn't I? I went out there to see Mr. Mason about a job. He gave me a dollar in town that day. I told him I was homeless, down on my luck, and he gave me a dollar and said come out and see him and maybe he could put me to work doing something on his farm. He told me his name and where he lived, said it was only about half a mile outside of town. So I walked out there that night. It was a hot night and I didn't have nothing to do in town, nowhere to go, no place to sleep, so I figured why not go out there and see Mr. Mason instead of waiting until the next day. I figured maybe he'd give me something to eat and a place to sleep. So I went out there. How was I to know he'd gone off to Springville on business and wouldn't be home until after midnight?

Well, I come onto his property about nine o'clock. Just after dark, so it must have been about nine. Wasn't nobody around, but lights was on in the house. It was a hot night, quiet, and when I got up near the porch I heard them sounds plain as day. Did I know right off what they was? Well, not right off. They was just moaning sounds to me at first, like maybe somebody was hurt. So I went around the side of the house, through the garden, to see if that was what it was, somebody hurt. That's how come you found my footprint over by the bedroom window, where I stepped in the mud from the sprinklers. I never said I wasn't in the garden, did I? But I never went up close to that window. No, sir. I'll swear it on a Bible. I never went close to that window and I never looked inside that bedroom.

I recognized them sounds, that's why. I knowed then what was going on. Him and her in there, making all that moaning noise, making them bedsprings squeak and squeal like a soul in torment. I knowed what they was doing. So I beat it right out of there, you bet I did. Fast.

Did I know it wasn't Mr. Mason in there with Mrs. Mason? Well, I guess I did. I guess I knowed it, all right. I heard the fellow's voice plain, some of the things he was saying to her . . . no, I ain't going to say what them things was. I don't even want to repeat them things in my own mind, let alone out loud. But I heard his voice plain and it wasn't Mr. Mason's voice so I guess I knowed it wasn't Mr. Mason in there. But I didn't know who it *was*. She didn't call him by his name. No, sir, not by his *name*.

No, I didn't go back to town right away. I told you that. It was a hot night and I didn't feel like going back to town right away, on account of what was I going to do once I got there? I didn't have no money or no place to go. What I did, I walked down by the river. River runs close to Mr. Mason's farm—runs right through a corner of it, didn't you say? Well, it was a hot night and I thought maybe I'd go for a swim.

But before I got there I seen this car parked in amongst the trees betwixt the river and Mr. Mason's house. Big fancy car, parked right in there under the trees, off the road so you couldn't see it unless you was walking by like I was. Well, I knowed it was his car, the fellow in the house with Mrs. Mason. Who else's car was it likely to be?

Sure, I looked inside. Door was unlocked, so I figured I might's well. But it wasn't my intention to steal nothing, even if there'd been something to steal. Which there wasn't. Big fancy car like that and not a thing in it that anybody'd want to steal. Not a thing you could of got fifty cents for at a hock shop, let alone a few dollars to buy you a decent meal and some new shoes and maybe a room to sleep in for a few nights.

I sure *didn't* wait there for him to show up. No, sir, you're wrong about that. I went on down to the river just like I said before. I went on down to the river and took off my clothes, all except my underpants, and I went for a nice cool swim. Then I laid on the bank a while and dried off. It was peaceful there on the bank, and I thought I'd stay right there the whole night. No point in going back to town, I says to myself. Might's well just stay right there for the night and then in the morning go and see if Mr. Mason had come home from wherever he was and ask him for that job he promised. I didn't have no intention of telling him about his wife fornicating with some other man. Not if he give me a job like he promised, and a place to sleep. I wouldn't hurt a good man that way. No, not a *good* man, I wouldn't.

Why didn't I spend the night there? Why'd I go on back to town instead? Well, I told you—I found that money. Eighty-nine dollars. Lying right there on the river bank. Way I found it was, I decided to take a walk along the bank, after I dried off from my swim, and see could I find some soft grass for a bed. And there that money was, in a little cloth purse that somebody must of dropped. Some fisherman or somebody. Dropped it right there on the bank and never realized it. There was a bright moon that night, you remember? That's how I seen the purse with the money in it lying there in the grass.

After I took the money out I throwed the bag in the river. I told you about that too. What did I want to keep an empty purse for? It didn't have no identification or nothing in it. Finders keepers, losers weepers. So I walked back into town with that found money. I figured I might's well spend some of it. I figured I was entitled, being as how I'd been down on my luck so long. So I bought myself a good meal and a bottle of bourbon whiskey and a room for the night, where you fellows found me the next morning.

What's that? No, sir, I sure didn't steal that money from Thomas Harper's wallet. I told you where I got that money. I found that money in a cloth purse lying on the river bank—

No, sir, I didn't hit Thomas Harper over the head with no chunk of willow limb. I didn't kill Thomas Harper. I never even knowed his name until you told me, or that he was a bigshot lawyer, or nothing about him except he was sinning with Mr. Mason's wife.

My fingerprints? Not just on his car but on one of them little window things in his wallet? Well, I don't know how they could have got *there*. You sure them fingerprints is mine too? Well, I don't know how they could of got there.

No, sir, I didn't rob and kill Thomas Harper.

No, sir, I didn't.

I tell you, I didn't do it . . .

All right. All right, all right. I guess it's no use. I guess I might's as well tell you.

I done it.

But I didn't mean to kill him, nor even to rob him. I come walking back from the river, back toward that fancy car of his, and I had that chunk of willow limb in my hand. I don't know why I picked it up down on the river bank. I just did, that's all. And here he comes from Mr. Mason's house where he'd been fornicating with Mr. Mason's wife, all cheerful and whistling, real pleased with himself, and I don't know . . . I don't know, I just stepped up behind him and let him have it. I didn't mean to hit him so hard. I truly didn't.

Sure, I took the money afterwards. Eighty-nine dollars is a lot of money to a fellow down on his luck. But that ain't why I hit him. I don't know why I hit him.

Yes I do. He had it coming, that's why. Sinning with Mr. Mason's wife like that, saying all them things to her right there in Mr. Mason's bed in Mr. Mason's own house. That Thomas Harper had it coming, all right.

But I *didn't* do that other thing. I swear I didn't.

I never looked through the bedroom window when I was in the garden, I never watched them two in Mr. Mason's bed. It's a mortal sin for a man to fornicate with another man's wife, and only a person with lust in his heart would gaze upon what he's moral certain is a act of fornication. God knows I don't have no lust in my heart and He knows I didn't watch them two committing their mortal sin. You got to know it too. You got to believe me.

I didn't do it!

Quicker Than the Eye

(with Michael Kurland)

When I returned from the dressing area at the rear of the Magic Cellar nightclub, the houselights were dimming for Christopher Steele's grand finale. I sat down quietly at the corner table I shared with four of the top brass of Lorde's Department Store ("Serving San Franciscans Since 1927"), and watched Steele raise his hand to cut off thunderous applause.

He waited until the room became completely silent. Then he said, "Thank you, ladies and gentlemen. You have been very attentive to my small displays of illusion, and I feel you should be rewarded. I shall show you something that is impossible, something that cannot be done. You are about to witness an effect that you will wonder about and talk about for the rest of your lives. You will tell people about it, and they will not believe you; but you will have seen it with your own eyes." He paused, smiling enigmatically. "I would appreciate your silence for the next ten minutes."

Steele bowed and stepped back to center stage. Ardis, his assistant—who had been with him longer than I had been his manager—joined him. They stood facing the audience, fingertips touching, while two stagehands brought in an ornate golden chair and placed it at the rear of the stage.

"The greatest mystery of all," Steele said, "is the mystery of time. Time and its effect on Man. The mystery of aging, of life and death. I present to you now a visual allegory and, if I may, a miracle!"

He stepped forward, and Ardis, at his nod, walked to the

high-backed chair and sat. The lights dimmed to a single spot.

"Ladies and gentlemen," Steele intoned, "please keep your seats and do not be alarmed at what you see here now. I invoke the aid of Osiris, Egyptian God of Life. Oh mighty Osiris, keeper of the mysteries, guardian of the keys, make your presence felt—on this stage tonight. Come forth, come here, come—now!"

Slowly, so slowly that you weren't really sure that it was happening, Ardis began to change. She slumped over in her seat and her arms and hands became lined and wrinkled. Her legs grew twisted, gnarled. Her face became ancient beyond the ages of Man, as old as Time.

She straightened up and stared out at the audience, this incredibly old hag, and her eyes flashed, even sunken as they were in the parchment of that ancient face. As we watched, the very flesh became transparent, the white dress she wore grew evanescent—and both disappeared, revealing the skeleton beneath. Finally the skeleton was all that remained. Then it collapsed in on itself, leaving only a pile of bones and a handful of dust on the chair.

"Thank you, ladies and gentlemen, for your attention," Steele said, as the lights went up and broke the spell. "That ends my show for tonight."

The audience stared. The chair, with bones and dust, remained. Finally one man began to clap and again everyone broke into thunderous applause. As it died down Steele smiled and clapped his hands twice, sharply. There was a flash of light, a puff of smoke, and Ardis—young and beautiful—stood once more beside him. This broke up the audience completely. They whistled, stamped and screamed while Steele and Ardis bowed low and then walked off the stage.

The houselights came up and the waitress appeared by the table with a fresh round of drinks. I gave my attention to my guests.

Old Mrs. Lorde herself sat opposite me, straight as a mannequin despite her eighty-plus years. She wore a severe black dress accented only by a massive gold choker. An ebony cane with a solid-gold handle cast in the shape of an elephant was her only other adornment. On my left were Victor Schneider, manager of Lorde's Department Store—a tall, stately man with a small moustache—and Lillian Royce, buyer in the women's clothing department and a very attractive brunette in her mid-twenties. On my right was a thin nervous man with a voice that just managed not to squeak: Lewis Thorp, the store's assistant manager.

"That was quite a performance," Schneider said, sampling his drink, a Magic Cellar specialty called a Levitation. "Quite a performance indeed."

Mrs. Lorde concurred. "I must say, I am very impressed with Mr. Steele. His act will be good for Lorde's image as well as for business. Very dignified and impressive. At first, you know, when I heard about this after returning from Europe last week, I thought it was cheap and vulgar publicity."

She was talking about Steele's next engagement, which was to spend two weeks in a hermetically sealed, glass-topped coffin in Lorde's front window—beginning tonight. The idea had been Steele's originally, but after many weeks of subtle talks I had managed to convince Schneider that *he* had thought of it. A good theatrical manager is a good con man.

"My late husband, you know," Mrs. Lorde continued, "was very fond of magicians. He'd seen the Great Carter as a youth and it impressed him greatly. Of course, watching magicians was only a minor passion compared to his love of stamps."

Schneider looked at his watch. "Speaking of Mr. Lorde's stamps," he said, "I'd better call McCarthy. I want to make sure of the time he and his men are coming to move the collection."

Ian McCarthy was curator of the Lorde's Collection, one of the finest of United States issues in the world, featuring the only mint copy of the Hayes Two-and-a-Half-Cent Vermilion, probably the most valuable presidential portrait in existence. The entire issue was believed to have been destroyed in the San Francisco earthquake until, in 1929, this single stamp was found in the drawer of a desk being auctioned off by the post office. Mr. Lorde bought the stamp at auction for $22,000—an incredible price for the time—in honor of his wife who was distantly related to Lucy Webb Hayes, the President's wife.

The collection was periodically moved from one to another of the sixteen state-wide branches of Lorde's—tonight it was going to Sacramento, as usual late at night with top security precautions—and, as you'd expect, it brought in many an admiring philatelist. The main branch here in San Francisco maintained a stamp room which dispensed both rare and common stamps to eager buyers—the practical approach. Old man Lorde had been a hard-nosed businessman as well as a collector.

"Perhaps you had better go over to the store immediately," Mrs. Lorde said to Schneider. Her voice had a hard edge to it, as it had all night when she'd addressed him. I had the feeling she was not exactly pleased with her manager, for some reason.

"Yes, perhaps I should," Schneider said. He stood and offered me his hand. He was one of those people who think politeness is what separates Man from the Lower Orders. Lillian Royce seemed to think this was an admirable quality.

When Schneider had given Miss Royce a radiant smile and departed, Lewis Thorp leaned toward me and said in his high voice, "Tell me, Booth, how does Steele do that aging trick?"

Trying not to wince at the word "trick," I cupped my hand to my mouth confidentially. "Magic," I whispered.

Lillian Royce giggled.

Steele was sitting in front of the triple mirror removing his makeup when I entered his dressing room minutes later. "Beautiful show," I said. "You left them breathless."

"Thank you, Matthew." He began to don the outfit he would wear in the coffin for the next two weeks: black pants, black turtleneck sweater, black jacket, very somber and correct for a coffin with a glass top. "Have the Lorde's people left for the store?" he asked.

I said they had. "There's a limousine waiting for us out front."

"Was the coffin delivered?"

"Yes. Thorp told me it arrived around six." I had been at Steele's house across the bay in Berkeley at three, when the movers had picked up the apparatus from his basement workshop.

"I don't know what I'd do without you, Matthew," he said. With his thick black hair, dark complexion, and deep-set eyes, the all-black costume made him look somewhat sinister.

Ardis joined us, wearing a simple white dress as provocative as any of her stage costumes; her long, auburn hair was now arranged in a precise manner. She linked her arm familiarly through Steele's and we walked out to the waiting limousine. Ardis lived in a private wing of Steele's enormous house, and was his closest friend and confidante. If there were any other quality to their relationship, only they knew of it.

The limousine took us swiftly and silently through a foggy San Francisco night to Post Street. Lorde's main entrance was floodlit, and there was a large crowd on hand. The publicity I had planted in articles, columns, and local TV shows had paid off.

Steele and Ardis waved to the crowd and hurried inside the store; it was 9:50 and the entombment was set for ten o'clock. I would have gone in with them, but the security guard at the door wouldn't let me pass. The store was isolated except for a few top employees because of the collection. I went over to the window to see how the coffin looked in place. On a two-foot marble pedestal, set about five feet back from the floor-to-ceiling window and parallel to it, the coffin was of dark, polished wood. Inside, through the thick glass top, you could see the white satin lining Steele would be lying on for the next two weeks. The angle, and a couple of lights inside the coffin, gave a clear view of the inside and of Steele, once he entered. When the glass top was set in place, the crack would be sealed with hot wax, presently bubbling on a brazier to the left of the coffin.

The only other items in the window were a large calendar to record the passage of the days of Steele's entombment, a large clock to tick off the seconds, minutes, and hours, and two posters in the Houdini style of flamboyance—gaudy electric-blue and yellowish-red announcements of the greatness of Christopher Steele, which were behind the coffin.

Mrs. Lorde and Victor Schneider entered the window, followed by Steele, Ardis, and a committee of four reputable citizens who would examine the coffin and pour the wax to seal the lid and deprive Steele of his air supply. In the eleven years I've been with Steele I've seen maybe a hundred of these committees, and there hasn't been one yet which could spot a gaff unless it reached up and popped them on the nose. Their chances of spotting this gaff—the gimmick that enabled Steele to work the effect—were exactly zero. As a matter of fact, so were mine; Steele had refused to allow me to examine the coffin while he was working on it.

Steele gave an introductory speech to the crowd via microphone and loudspeaker while the committee probed and prodded at the coffin. He explained how fakirs of the East had developed techniques for shallow breathing that enabled them to live for extended periods of time with little oxygen. He told of the years he had spent mastering this technique and that of slowing his heartbeat. Then he climbed into the coffin and the glass lid was lowered into place. Schneider and one of the committee members poured the molten wax into the groove around the lid. Steele now had maybe five hours of air left. Two weeks is three hundred and thirty-six hours . . .

"How does he do it?" a voice asked behind me; it was Lillian Royce. "These tricks of his, I mean, like that scary thing in the Magic Cellar where the girl turns into a skeleton?"

I had the feeling that she wanted to talk to someone about anything at all, and I was there and the effects were a convenient topic. I'm always willing to talk with a beautiful woman, and the effects are not really secret, just sort of confidential.

"First of all," I said, drawing her to one side, "don't ever call them tricks. They're effects, or slights, or illusions, but *never* tricks." I could see Steele's face at the extreme angle I was standing, but no more of him. It seemed to shimmer slightly by some illusion of the lighting as I turned away.

"Tell me," Lillian insisted, "how does he do it?"

"I warn you," I said, "magic is funny in one way: when it's explained it seems silly and obvious, no matter how powerful the effect was when you saw it. That's why magicians never explain their effects. You're being fooled, and people resent being fooled."

"I can't figure it out," Lillian said. "I admit he's fooled me."

"It's called the Blue Room Illusion," I told her. "Maybe fifty years old. It involves a peculiar optical property of glass."

"What's that?"

"If a plate of perfectly clear glass is dark on one side and well lit on the other, it turns into a mirror on the lighted side. You've probably noticed this on windows at night."

"Where was the glass?" Lillian asked.

"Picture the stage," I told her. "Ardis comes in wearing that sexy white dress and goes to the chair at the back. The lights dim except for a couple of spots on her. Steele goes into his spiel. That's when it happens. A sheet of clear plate glass—a giant, damned expensive sheet of clear plate glass—is slid into place on concealed tracks diagonally across the stage. It's invisible to the audience because it's meticulously cleaned and evenly lighted on both sides.

"Then, slowly, the lights on the far side of the glass are lowered and the lights on this side"—I wiggled my fingers to indicate which side—"are raised. The glass turns into a mirror, reflecting the image of an identical chair at right angles to the stage, concealed in the wings. An assistant in a copy of Ardis' costume, made up to look incredibly ancient, is sitting in the chair. The gradual change of lights makes it look as though Ardis herself is aging."

Lillian looked incredulous. "What about the skeleton?"

"While Ardis is in darkness she gets out of the chair and is replaced by the skeleton. Then the lights change again and the glass is silently slid back."

"Gosh," Ardis said, appearing behind me with an armful of posters, "I thought it was magic."

"Ardis," I said, "meet Lillian Royce. She buys."

"Indeed?" Ardis said. "Excuse me." She pushed through the crowd and began tacking up display posters on one of the wooden boards framing the exterior of the window. They were identical to the yellow-red ones inside, behind the coffin.

I turned back to Lillian. "I've just had a brilliant idea," I said. "Why don't we—"

A sudden loud flapping sound cut off the rest of what I was going to say, and Lillian and I and the rest of the crowd shifted our gaze to Ardis and her poster. She had slipped: tacked up the top of the poster, stretched out the bottom, and then let go. The poster had, of course, rolled back up.

"The unflappable Ardis," I said to Lillian. "Well, there's always a first time. As I was about to ask you, why don't we go over to Franscatti's and get something to eat?"

"I'd love to," Lillian said.

"Sounds good," a new high-pitched voice cut in, and Lewis Thorp appeared at my elbow. "You won't mind if I join you?"

I was trying to figure out how to answer that politely when Mrs. Lorde emerged from the front door and saved me the trouble. "Mr. Thorp," she called, waving her cane at us, "I wish to see you. You too, Miss Royce." She looked disturbed, angry. "Will you both come up to my office, please. I won't keep you long, Miss Royce."

"The Queen Mother calls," Thorp said.

"Do you mind going on ahead?" Lillian asked me. "I'll join you as soon as I can."

"As soon as she could" turned out to be about twenty minutes after I had arrived at Franscatti's, which caters to the late-night crowd. "I'm sorry. There were some things . . ." She sat down in the booth across from me, looking distracted and unhappy. "I couldn't find Victor," she said.

"Schneider? Why were you looking for him?"

"We're . . . friends," she said vaguely. "Something peculiar is going on, and I don't know what it is. Mrs. Lorde is angry, and Victor is . . . Oh, I don't know *where* Victor is."

"He's probably gone home to sleep, like any sensible man."

"No, I don't think so. He wouldn't leave the store until Mr. McCarthy came to move the stamps, and Mr. McCarthy hadn't arrived yet when I left. He's due any time."

"Well," I said, "I'm sure Schneider is around somewhere. There's no need to worry."

I ordered spaghetti with white clam sauce, and when it came it seemed to cheer Lillian up a bit. We started to talk of, among other things, my life as a magician's manager. "While Steele's lying in that coffin practicing shallow breathing or whatever," I said, "I'm going to be getting TV crews down to film it; keeping crowds in front of the window day and night; seeing that it's played up on local *and* national news. He lies there while I do all the work, which is why he's a genius and I work for him."

"Does he do this sort of thing often?" she asked.

"He doesn't like to repeat himself," I answered. "There're people who make a living just getting buried, but Steele is doing it because he's never done it before. It's a challenge, and he can't turn down a challenge of any kind. That's the way he is."

"Are these effects original?"

"Some are. In Steele's case there's something original in every effect—and his presentation is always original, created to fit his stage personality. Otherwise, it wouldn't be a challenge."

It was past 11:30 when we walked the three blocks back to

the store. The crowd was still there but its focus had shifted from the coffin in the window to the main door. Drawn up in front were three police cars, a couple of unmarked vehicles with red lights suction-cupped to their tops, and an ambulance.

Steele was snug in his coffin in the great window to the left of the entrance, serenely staring at the ceiling. After checking on him we pushed our way through the crowd. Judging by their conversation, none of them had any idea of what was going on.

A uniformed cop stood at the door, repelling traffic. When we gave him our names he let us in and told us to go up to the executive offices on the second floor. He wouldn't tell us anything else.

Mrs. Lorde was sitting in rigid solitude in the middle of a large Regency-for-the-masses couch, with both hands firmly twined around the butt of her gold-handled cane. Lewis Thorp sat in a hard-backed chair opposite, wearing an expression that indicated a submerged and unpleasant emotion. Also present were two stoic patrolmen.

"What happened here?" I demanded of the group at large.

Thorp looked over at me sourly, then switched his gaze to Lillian. "It's Schneider," he said. "He's been killed."

"Oh!" Lillian's hand went to her mouth, and all the blood drained out of her face. She managed to stumble over to the couch nearest us and drop onto it. She began to weep softly.

"Mr. McCarthy found him," Mrs. Lorde said. "In the Stamp Room." She proceeded to explain that when McCarthy and his men had arrived at the store, they hadn't been able to get into the Stamp Room because they couldn't locate Schneider, who had the only key. Mrs. Lorde had sent Schneider to the Stamp Room to do some last-minute inventorying, and insisted that was where he had to be. So, with her permission, McCarthy and his men had broken the door in. "He was lying on the floor in front of the sales counter," she finished. "Nothing they could do for him. Terrible thing. Terrible."

At that moment a man entered through the wide door to the executive-office area, and we all turned our attention to him. He was short and stocky and wearing a gray suit, the vest of which was buttoned over a blue shirt and old-school-stripe tie. "Sorry to keep you waiting so long," he said, "but there was some routine that had to be gone through first." He glanced at Lillian still sobbing on the couch, and then looked over at me. "You'd be Matthew Booth, is that right?"

"Yes," I said. "And you?"

"Lieutenant Garrett. Homicide."

"Was Victor Schneider's death accidental?" I asked him.

"Not likely. Medical examiner says he was struck in the throat by a blunt object about the size of a thumb, which pierced the skin and the thyroid cartilage, crushing said cartilage and closing the trachea. In plain English, he choked to death because he could no longer breathe. Nasty way to die."

Lillian had raised her head to listen, but now she made a keening sound—one of horror and grief—and lowered her face into her hands again. I thought of saying something to Garrett about his insensitivity, but then I realized he knew exactly what he was doing. He'd been watching Lillian and the rest of us closely as he talked.

"Perhaps it wasn't murder at all," a voice suggested, and I looked over to see Ardis had entered the room; I'd been wondering where she was. "Perhaps the poor man tripped and fell against that thumb-sized something you mentioned."

"I'm afraid not, Miss," Garrett said. "Any such object would have traces of blood, and there are none."

"Then you didn't find the weapon either?" I asked.

"Not yet. But it'll turn up eventually."

"If Schneider was murdered, who could have done it?"

"We don't make guesses," Garrett said, which meant he didn't have any idea who had done it. "Everyone in this room, it seems, has no concrete alibi for the time of death—except perhaps you, Mr. Booth. Anyone here could be guilty. Or none of you, for that matter. Although, as far as we can tell right now, no one else could have gotten into the store. And you few could play hide-and-seek for hours in this huge empty place."

"What about motive?" Ardis asked.

"After we talk to everyone here, maybe we'll know more along that line." Another noncommittal answer. "Our first thought, of course, was robbery, since the murder took place in the Stamp Room with the Lorde's Collection. But the collection appears to be intact; Mr. McCarthy is checking it now." He frowned. "We don't even know—yet—how the killer got into or out of the Stamp Room. The only key is still on Schneider's key ring; and the windows are barred with half-inch steel that hasn't been touched in thirty years."

So there it was: what appeared to be a locked-room murder. I thought of Steele downstairs in his glass-topped coffin (the murder would spell the end of his two-week planned illusion; Lorde's now had all the publicity it could handle, whether negative or positive). But Steele wouldn't be too upset, I knew. Puzzles fascinated him; the more bizarre a puzzle was, the better he liked it. The man thrived on challenges, as I'd told Lillian earlier. Consequently life was never dull around Christopher Steele—but this was the first time I knew of a murder being part of the amalgam.

"I'd better go look at Christopher," Ardis said. "He must be curious to find out what's going on outside his little glassed-in world."

"You'll have to do it from inside, Miss," Garrett said. "The uniformed officers at the door have orders not to let anyone out."

"Really!" Mrs. Lorde said. "You don't think any of us are going to run away?"

"It's not that," Garrett explained. "We may want to search each of you before you leave."

"Looking for what?"

"We don't know yet."

"I'll stay inside," Ardis assured the lieutenant, and headed off toward the escalator.

"Why," Garrett asked, "does she want to look at him?"

"I think she wants *him* to look at *her,*" I explained. "They have a sign language they use for a mind-reading act. You see—"

"Incredible! Absolutely incredible!"

We turned around. A small, gray man had appeared at the door and was waving a magnifying glass about. "Incredible! Who would have thought such? Impossible! Not even gummed!"

We all stared at each other while the lieutenant strode over to the little man. "Calm yourself, Mr. McCarthy. What is it?"

McCarthy thrust something tiny into Garrett's face. "Here," he said. "Look at this!"

"It's a stamp?" Lieutenant Garrett asked.

"It is not! When you asked me to go through the stamps I said to myself this is a waste of time, a complete waste of time . . ."

"You said it to us too, Mr. McCarthy."

"I was mistaken. It's incredible. This is the Hayes Two-and-a-Half-Cent Vermilion. But it *isn't.* It's an imitation. And not even gummed! Looking at it through the glass, even an expert might have missed it. Incredible!"

"What's the real stamp worth?" Garrett asked the old man.

"Priceless," McCarthy said. "Whatever someone will pay for it. It's one-of-a-kind."

"Well, what's it insured for?"

"I believe two hundred thousand dollars. But you understand its intrinsic value could be much higher, depending upon just how badly someone else wanted the stamp."

"It looks like someone wanted it pretty badly," Garrett said. "Let's get that magician up here."

"You don't think—" I started.

Garrett looked at me. "What don't I think?"

"Christopher Steele couldn't have anything to do with this," I said. "He's been locked in a coffin in plain view of a crowd of people since ten o'clock."

"That may be," Garrett said, "but he's the only one who was in the store at the time of the murder who isn't here now, so we might as well have him. Maybe he can give us a little insight into locked rooms—professionally, that is."

"I'd be delighted, Lieutenant," Steele's deep stage voice said behind us. We turned and saw him standing in the doorway with Ardis.

"Where the hell did you come from?" Garrett demanded.

"Ardis told me what was happening. I had her break the wax seal around the lid and let me out."

"It was all news to you, was it?"

Steele smiled faintly. "I've been sealed inside that coffin for the past three hours, Lieutenant. I did see the arrival of the police vehicles, of course, but I had no idea what had happened."

"I'd like to have a close look at that coffin of yours," Garrett said. "Unless you have objections?"

"Certainly not." Steele's eyes began to gleam. "Did I understand you to say you'd like me to examine the locked room where the murder took place?"

Garrett thought about it. "That might be an idea," he said. "You ever use a locked-room gimmick in your act?"

"Various effects that could be applied to a seemingly locked room," Steele said. "But remember, there is no such thing as a 'locked room' in the sense we're using the term. People cannot walk through walls."

I suppressed a chuckle, and Steele glared at me. One of his best effects is to have masons come on stage and build a brick wall in full view of the audience. Then Steele proceeds to pass through it. Houdini invented that one.

Steele shifted his gaze back to the lieutenant. "Can I see that room now?"

"All right. It can't hurt anything. In fact, why don't we all adjourn to the Stamp Room. The lab crew's gone by now."

So all of us went down to the Stamp Room. There was a chalk outline where the body had lain on the worn maroon carpeting, but nothing else seemed out of place. Jutting out from the wall on the right were eight display cases filled with trays of stamps and envelopes, with printed cards telling what each was and in some instances giving historical data. At the rear was a long glass counter with stamps, stamp albums, books about stamps; these were the items for sale by Lorde's. On the counter top was a telephone, several reference books, catalogs, a charge-card machine, and some pencils. The left side of the room had three eight-foot-high shelves, like stacks in a library, running parallel to the wall with the door; these had trays of stamps and first covers, some of which were for sale and some of which belonged to the Lorde's Collection. The windows were directly opposite, behind the counter. Not only were the bars firmly in place, but the sash was painted to the frame.

Steele walked to the middle of the room and turned in a slow circle, studying everything in it, and I knew that the single turnaround had fixed every detail of the Stamp Room in his mind.

He stared at the counter briefly, turned and walked to the display cases on the right. "Where was the stamp?" he asked.

"Third case from the rear," McCarthy told him. "Incredible!"

"We'll worry about the stamp later," Garrett said. "Well, Steele? Do you see anything we might have missed?" His voice was tinged with irony.

"Perhaps," Steele said. "Mr. McCarthy, what did you do when you found the body?"

"I left the room and called the police."

"You didn't touch anything in here?"

"I know better than that."

"You didn't call from this phone?"

"No. I didn't want to disturb anything."

Steele nodded and turned to Garrett. "You said the room was locked from the inside. Surely there are cylinders on both sides of the door?" With his air of positive command, it didn't occur to the detective that he should be asking the questions and Steele responding. Steele's carefully nurtured stage personality had some use away from the footlights.

"There are," Garrett admitted. "But there's only one key, and it's supposed to be in the possession of the manager at all times, because of insurance regulations. It was found in his pocket."

"May I see it, please?"

Garrett asked another officer to get the "evidence envelope," and the man nodded and left the room. "We'll find the killer," the lieutenant said to Steele. "But to make a case, we have to know how he got out of the room. Can you tell us?"

Steele offered his hand. "I accept the challenge."

Garrett, who was unaware that he had issued a challenge, shook hands—and then frowned.

"This isn't a publicity thing, is it? It better not be. I want no statements to the press unless you clear with me first."

"No publicity, I assure you, Lieutenant. The challenge of the puzzle itself is my reward. Just give me access to the information as you collect it, and I promise you the mystery will be satisfactorily solved. As I said before, there's no such thing as a locked room."

The officer came back with a large manila envelope and handed it to Garrett, who ripped it open and dumped the items inside onto a glass counter. "Schneider's pockets, contents of," he said.

Steele picked up the key ring and isolated and examined the Stamp Room key. "Not copied recently," he told Garrett, "and no impression taken."

"How do you know?"

"Simple," Steele said. "Your laboratory will say the same. If it had been copied there would be some sign of it on the lands, where the copying pantograph would be pressed against it. If it had been impressed, then some miniscule particle of wax or clay would have adhered to the inner surface of this groove."

"All right, Steele," Garrett said. "You see anything else there?"

"Not at the moment," Steele answered, but his eyes had a secretive look that I recognized. He was onto something, and he wasn't ready to share it. Steele has a flair for the dramatic and, on occasion, the melodramatic, and his timing is excellent.

There was a point that was bothering me, and I decided to ask: "Doesn't this room have a burglar alarm?"

Garrett nodded. “It does, but not on the door.”

“That’s right,” Thorp said. “The alarm system is wired into the display cases. It sets off a silent alarm in the office of the private security outfit we use.”

“Then why didn’t the alarm go off when the Hayes stamp was stolen?” I asked.

Garrett turned to Thorp. “That’s a damn good question. Where’s the alarm control box?”

“Outside in Sportswear. In a recessed wall cubicle.”

“Who has the keys?”

Thorp colored slightly. “Key; there’s only one. I have it. One of my duties is to activate the alarm system after closing.”

“Let’s see it.”

Thorp pulled it from his pocket. It was a single key, too large to fit on any ring; about as long as a fountain pen, and thicker around, with an irregular series of grooves on one end and a large round handle on the other.

“Fascinating,” Steele said, taking it from Thorp’s hand and examining it. “It must be over thirty years old.”

“The alarm system is older than that,” Thorp said. “We’ve been taking bids on modernizing it.”

“This thing must be a chore to carry around.” Steele hefted the key. “It’s solid brass—and look how shiny it is.”

“I usually keep it in the safe. Only take it out to turn the system on and off.”

“How do you get into the store without setting off the alarm, then?” Garrett asked.

“I don’t. The alarm covers the entrance doors, and it goes off when the first person comes into the store in the morning. He has to call the security people immediately and identify himself. It’s usually me or Mr. Schneider. Then I reset the alarm.”

"Who else has the combination to the safe?"

"Victor Schneider had," Thorp said. "Only he."

"That poses a question," Garrett said. "Thorp here could have turned off the alarm, but he couldn't get into the room."

"Are you suggesting—" Thorp's face flushed dark red.

"Just speculating," Lieutenant Garrett said. "It's my job. Now, Schneider could have come in here and turned off the alarm, but then we'd have to assume he had an accomplice, since he didn't murder himself."

"Didn't he have to have the alarm off to inventory the stamps?" Mrs. Lorde asked. "That's what he was doing. I asked him to do the first inventory, then Mr. McCarthy would do the second. We always do two."

"It's a physical inventory," McCarthy said. "He didn't have to touch them or examine them, just make sure they were there. He just peered through the glass."

"One second," Steele said. He disappeared down one of the short aisles between the display cases on the right. "Is this the inventory control sheet?" he asked, coming back out with a clipboard in his hand.

"Yes," McCarthy said.

"Where did you find it?" Garrett demanded.

"On top of the case, about halfway along. It's checked off to item number three-twenty-six. Where would that be?"

"Right about where you found the clipboard," McCarthy said.

"So Schneider got it in the middle of his inventory," Garrett mused.

"He caught someone stealing the stamp," Thorp said.

"How was the stamp stolen without the alarm going off?"

"A duplicate key could have been made," I volunteered. "Someone could have taken an impression of the lock; it's right out there in plain view of any customer with a piece of wax."

Steele glared at me. "It's not that easy. *I* could have done it, but that's my profession and I've had twenty years' practice. Few amateurs could have done it."

"Well, a man is dead and a valuable stamp is missing," Garrett said. "Somebody did something. Now, if you don't mind, I'd like to question each of you separately. Miss Royce, I understand that you and Mr. Schneider were good friends."

Lillian nodded her assent. She still seemed dazed.

"Would you come with me, please?" Garrett asked gently. "Let's talk about it." He led her out of the Stamp Room and we all more or less straggled behind. Garrett preempted the private office for interrogation, with Mrs. Lorde's grudging permission.

Steele called Ardis over to us. "Are you still friendly with that young lady who works for the phone company?"

"As far as I know," she said.

"Get hold of her. Find an open phone. Tell her—"

"But it's—"

"I know, it's three o'clock in the morning. We'll take her out to dinner next week. Have her get over to the billing computer and get a list of all numbers called from this store since ten o'clock this evening."

Ardis went off. Magicians' assistants are used to doing whatever their boss asks of them without question and without hesitation. It's a necessary prerequisite of the job; otherwise one of them can wind up embarrassed, injured, or dead.

Magicians' managers, however, are another matter. "Why do you want the list of numbers?" I asked Steele.

He gave me one of his enigmatic smiles. "Perhaps we'll

find nothing, and perhaps a great deal," he said.

"Thanks a lot."

Steele walked over to where Mrs. Lorde was leaning on her cane, scowling down at the floor. "I wonder if I might ask you a few questions," he said.

She lifted her head and regarded him with one eye. "What questions, young man?"

"I'll be brief. I imagine you must be distressed by the death of Mr. Schneider and the loss of the Hayes Two-and-a-Half-Cent Vermilion."

"The stamp is insured," Mrs. Lorde said. "A man's life is infinitely more important than a piece of gummed paper. Even a man like Victor Schneider."

Steele raised an eyebrow. "Meaning?"

"Meaning Victor Schneider was a fool and an incompetent. If he had not died, I would almost certainly have replaced him."

"Incompetent as a store manager?"

"Indeed. His accounting procedures were dangerous and he had a knack for purchasing unsalable merchandise without consulting anyone. If I had not been in Europe for more than a year, I would have discovered this much sooner."

"How long had Schneider been your manager here?"

"A little over two years."

"I see," Steele said. "Did you have someone in mind as his replacement?"

"Of course. Lewis Thorp."

"Did Thorp know of your displeasure with Schneider? Did he know that he was next in line?"

"He did not. I tell no one what I intend to do until I do it. However, I did plan to speak to Lewis about Schneider tonight; that is why I summoned him to my office earlier. There were interruptions and then this murder and theft, so I did not have the chance to carry out my intention."

"You hadn't as yet mentioned to Schneider that his job was in jeopardy, is that correct?"

"It is. I was waiting until our CPA firm completed an independent audit this past week, but when I had their report, I knew nothing more than I had previously. There are incompetents in every business. So I called a second CPA firm; they will begin *their* audit next week."

"You suspected a shortage, Mrs. Lorde? Embezzlement?"

She tapped her cane sharply on the hardwood floor. "Not exactly. Victor Schneider was a fool but not a knave; he lacked the intellectual capacity for knavery. No, I merely suspect mismanagement due to incompetence. But our CPA's are also incompetent. They couldn't tell, they said, if there were any discrepancies. Do you believe that? Well, I expect the new firm I've hired *will* be able to tell."

Steele nodded thoughtfully.

"I suppose you think it's rude of me to speak so harshly of the dead," Mrs. Lorde said, "but Death is too close a companion for me to hold in reverence."

"A man in death is just what he was in life," Steele said sententiously. "Neither more nor less, and he should be remembered thus." He gave the old woman a courtly bow, and we turned away.

I studied his face, and he had the air of someone doing mental mathematics. He said, "Tell me, Matthew, about your friend, Miss Royce. Have you any idea of her feelings toward Lewis Thorp?"

I thought back to my dinner conversation with Lillian. The subject had come up, briefly. "He made a pass at her once, which she repulsed. Subsequently he got himself a steady girlfriend and ignored Lillian—Miss Royce. She happily ignored him also."

Steele fell silent, pondering again as he led the way to Lewis Thorp's office cubicle.

Thorp was sitting at his desk. He looked up and gave us a wan smile as we approached. "Well, Mr. Steele," he said, "any new developments?"

Steele shook his head. "I'd like to hear your ideas."

"If you mean about how poor Victor was murdered in a locked room," Thorp said, "I can't help you. It seems like a baffling crime."

"So it does," Steele agreed.

"Victor must have been killed by whoever stole the stamp," Thorp said. "He must have walked in on him—the thief, I mean."

"That's not likely," Steele said. "He would have known that the theft would be uncovered in the murder investigation."

"Maybe he just wanted time to get the stamp out."

"No, I don't think the theft has anything to do with the murder. Just an unfortunate coincidence."

Thorp worried his lower lip for a moment. "There *is* one other possibility," he said. "Our books have just undergone a surprise audit. The rumor is that there was a major discrepancy."

"You think Schneider may have been tapping the till?"

"I knew Victor rather well. He had his faults, as we all do, but he seemed to be a basically honest man. But he *was* extravagant in his tastes, and he *may* have needed money. If he was embezzling from the store and someone found out about it, he may have tried to blackmail him. And suppose they had a fight of some kind, and Schneider was killed by accident. Or suppose he had an accomplice who thought that the audit would reveal Schneider's duplicity and killed to keep himself in the clear."

"How could such an embezzlement have been accomplished?" Steele asked.

Thorp considered. "What was done—if anything at all was done—was probably a juggling of purchase records; false requisitions to dummy firms, with the money paid by Lorde's siphoned off. That's done to firms like ours periodically; we have to be on the watch for it. And any one of a dozen people in the store might have helped Schneider falsify records."

"I see. It's an interesting theory, in any case. I appreciate your candor, Mr. Thorp."

Thorp nodded, and Steele and I left him in his cubicle. When we returned to the front area, I saw that Ardis had come up from downstairs and was beckoning across the floor to us. Steele went immediately to meet her. I was about to follow, but Lillian Royce appeared and intercepted me, clutching at my arm.

"I . . . I'd like to speak with you, Matthew," she said. Her nails dug into the tweed of my jacket.

"Of course."

"I know I shouldn't impose, but . . . there's no one else I can talk to just now about Victor."

I took her hand. "I understand," I said.

"I've just come from a long talk with Lieutenant Garrett. I did most of the talking. He kept asking questions. I told him the truth, that I was having an affair with Victor. Everyone seemed to know that already. Victor was a nice man, you know. Ineffectual, weak, easily taken advantage of—but he meant well, he always meant well. And they seem to think I might have killed him. Why would I want to kill Victor? Why would anyone—?" She broke off abruptly and buried her face against my shoulder. I could feel her tears against my neck, but she didn't make a sound. I held her.

It was perhaps two silent minutes later when Steele and

Ardis came over to us. "I dislike interrupting," he said quietly, "but you could help me if you would, Miss Royce."

Lillian took a deep breath, and then stepped away from me and faced Steele.

He said, "Matthew mentioned your describing Mr. Thorp's acquisition of an inamorata—a girlfriend. Do you know her?"

"Yes," Lillian answered. "Ginny Epworth."

Steele nodded again. Just then Lieutenant Garrett came out of the private office. "Oh, Steele!" he called, then waited until he reached us to continue: "One of our lab men has a farfetched theory on how the killer got into and out of the Stamp Room, but I'd like you to hear it anyway."

"I don't have to, Lieutenant," Steele said. "I know how it was done."

"What?"

"And I believe I can name the killer of Victor Schneider."

My mouth, I think, dropped open. So did Garrett's. There was a silence; then Garrett said warily, "Go ahead."

"My proof is, at the moment, merely inferential," Steele said. "But if you will bear with me, I believe I can suggest a means for establishing the killer's identity."

"Just name him."

"If you would join us in the Stamp Room, and bring the others with you—and if you would then give me ten minutes to propound a little scenario—I'll give him to you."

"Just *name* him," Garrett repeated.

"It wouldn't do you any good; you couldn't arrest him. Give me ten minutes, and I guarantee you *can* arrest him."

"I can't authorize you to ask any questions in the name of the Police Department."

"I won't be asking any."

Garrett thought it over, then shrugged. "You've got your ten minutes," he said.

We stood or sat on two sides of the Stamp Room, facing each other. Ardis, McCarthy, Lillian, and I were by the door, with a plainclothesman in the doorway. Across from us, Thorp, Mrs. Lorde, and Lieutenant Garrett were in front of the counter. Steele, of course, stood in the center of the room; it was his show.

"I would like to attempt an experiment," Steele said, slowly turning around, his eye catching and examining each of us in turn. "Before I do, I should tell you that there is no magic, nothing mystical in what I am about to do."

I suppressed a smile. Always watch a magician most closely when he tells you there is no trick. Steele had everyone else's complete attention.

"There is a psychic aura of the past that is always with us," Steele continued. "It seems to be strongest in the presence of death—particularly violent death. Some people believe that this psychic aura explains the phenomenon we call 'ghosts,' other experimenters equate it with that strange sense that what is happening has happened before: what the French call *deja vu*." Steele was using his intense, mellifluous, almost hypnotic stage voice on us, a voice which compelled suspension of disbelief until the effect—whatever he was after—was accomplished.

"With experience and help, a few sensitive people have been able to read this aura and unfold the story it conceals. I am going to attempt to do this in this room. I will need your help."

Mrs. Lorde was skeptical and impatient. "What is it you want us to do?" she asked.

"Patience," Steele said. "I am about to tell the story that I read in the psychic patterns of this room. I may appeal to one or more of you for help as I go along. Verbal help. That's all I require."

"Go on," Garrett said.

Steele raised his arms above his head. "Let us go back," he said. "Back almost four hours, to the act of murder and all that led up to it." He began prowling about the room, examining the walls, the windows, the display cases, the two aisles between the stacks, and even the floor—as though there were words written there for him to find. "I see this room," he said. "It is empty, waiting. Now Victor Schneider enters. He has come to inventory the stamps; he has a list in his hands and he is checking the stamps off against it, not really examining them but merely seeing that they are there.

"He checks the counter first. Then he goes over to the stacks . . ." Steele disappeared down one of the aisles, then returned and pointed dramatically at the door. "The murderer!" he announced. Everyone stared at the plainclothesman, who was blocking the doorway.

"The door slowly opens," Steele continued, his finger still pointing, "and the murderer enters. He closes the door behind him. I think—yes, he locks it."

"Now wait a minute," Garrett protested. "Schneider had the only key to the room—we know that."

"Do we?" Steele asked. "I told you, Lieutenant, that there is no such thing as a 'locked-room' mystery. The murderer had a key—a duplicate key no doubt made some time ago by Victor Schneider and foolishly given to the killer for the sake of expediency. The murderer used it to get in, and he locked the door with it when he left."

"Then where is it now?" Garrett demanded.

"I have no idea. Let me go on." Steele stared about the room again, as if to relocate the aura. "The killer is in the room. What does he do? Does he attack Victor Schneider? No. He doesn't see Schneider. He thinks he is alone. He advances—" Steele advanced "—to the counter. Is it the stamp he's after?"

Steele paused before the case that had held the Hayes Two-and-a-Half-Cent Vermilion and contemplated it. "No. There is no aura of violence about this case. It was something else. What?" He ran his hand a foot above the counter as though it were a sensitive antenna tuning in to the auric vibrations. The hand paused and quivered over the far right end of the counter. "The telephone," he said.

"What?" Garrett asked.

"He picked up the telephone. He dialed an outside number."

"What number? Who was he calling?"

"Why come in here to use the phone?" Lillian Royce asked. "There are fifty telephones in the store."

Steele pressed his hands to his forehead. His audience was obviously still with him, but I was beginning to wonder just what the hell he was doing. "I sense fear; fear, and a need for privacy. This person—the killer—locked himself in here to speak on the telephone of something so private that the overhearing of it was a mortal threat to him. Unfortunately for Victor Schneider, he did overhear this conversation."

Steele moved again to the stacks. "What exactly was it that Schneider overheard? The facts of a crime—yes, I sense a crime. Perhaps the killer was making plans with the person at the other end of the wire, plans for immediate escape with the ill-gotten gains of this crime, this theft . . ."

"The Vermilion!" Garrett said.

"No, not a stamp. Not a physical theft. Cheating or embezzling perhaps. Yes—and the killer was laboring under a misconception; he thought his crime had been discovered, that he faced a prison sentence, that his only alternative was to flee as quickly as possible."

Steele pointed a finger at the phone. "So Victor Schneider, overhearing all of this, decided to confront the person. And did so." He spread his hands, and then clapped them together. "Just so quickly are created a killer, and a corpse. No premeditation; just the sudden, overwhelming need to suppress a criminous act . . . Isn't that right—Lewis Thorp?"

Thorp looked startled, but not as startled as the rest of us; I guess he'd seen it coming. "What are you talking about?" he demanded, his voice harsh.

"There are records, you know, Mr. Thorp," Steele said, walking toward him. "The phone company must have a record of your call. And the person you called—" Steele held his hand above Thorp's head as though drawing forth thoughts "—the young lady you called . . . Miss Epworth."

Thorp brushed aside Steele's hand. "What is this? An accusation based on a damned mind-reading act? I don't have to put up with this. I called Ginny. Of course I called Ginny. Why shouldn't I?"

"From what phone?" Steele asked softly.

"What do you mean? How do I know what phone? I don't remember what phone."

"And the key, Mr. Thorp; how will you explain the key?"

"You mean to this room? I don't have a key to this room."

"But you know where it is, because you put it there," Steele said. "And I'm going to take you to it."

"You must be crazy," Thorp said, backing away.

"You're going to take my hand," Steele said, "and then *I'm* going to take *you* to the key—wherever it is."

We all watched, hypnotized, as Steele took hold of Thorp's wrist. "Come," he said, "let's go find that key. All you have to do is think about where it is, and I'll lead you to it." He pulled Thorp across the room, very much against Thorp's will. "And you can't help thinking about it, can you? That little brass key that nobody knew you had. Just lock the door behind you and hide the key and no one could ever prove you were in the room."

Steele literally pulled Thorp out of the room as he kept up the patter. We all followed behind at a respectful distance. Of course, now I knew what he was doing. It was very impressive on stage, and even more so now when it was being used to trap a murderer. "Just come along," Steele said, pulling Thorp by the wrist. "Which way? Where would you have put it? Over here?" He went to the left, toward the furniture department. "No, I think not." He turned to the right again, with Thorp behind him, still in his firm grasp. "Down here, I think. Surely not too far away, wouldn't want to get caught with it. Paused here to think, did you? Now down here? Ah—of course!" He stopped before a glass display case full of wallets and other leather goods. "Somewhere in here."

"This is ridiculous!" Thorp shouted, but there was panic in his voice. "What does it prove if there *is* a key in this case? You probably put it there yourself, Steele."

Steele smiled. "Do you really think that *I* would need a key to enter the Stamp Room, or any other room?"

Lillian came forward and slid the lock off the door to the case. Steele then opened the door with one hand, the other still firmly wrapped around Thorp's right wrist. "Where now?" he said, his hand running along the top of the various leather items. "I think . . . ah, yes!" He pulled a key holder from one of the trays. There were two keys in it for display, one brass and the other silver. "One of these," he said positively. He lifted the brass one by the ring. "This."

Lieutenant Garrett pushed forward. "Let me see that."

"Here you are, Lieutenant. Handle it gently. I think you'll find Mr. Thorp's fingerprints on it."

"What if it is my key?" Thorp's voice was higher and louder than he'd intended. "That doesn't prove anything!"

"Speaking of keys," Steele said to Garrett, "I suggest you examine the burglar-alarm key—which no one but Mr. Thorp uses, by his own admission—carefully under a microscope. You'll no doubt find traces of blood at the tip, even though Mr. Thorp scrubbed it bright before putting it in this case."

Of course! I thought. Thorp must have had the key in his possession when Schneider confronted him in the Stamp Room; this was the weapon, with its wide blunt tip, that he had in his fear driven into Schneider's throat.

Thorp realized, too, that he was trapped; that Garrett had all the evidence he needed now. His gaze dropped and he sagged in Steele's grasp. Lieutenant Garrett read him his rights, and he was handcuffed and taken away with no fuss at all.

Everyone was talking at once, looking at Steele as if he were some kind of wizard. When Garrett got them calmed down, he asked the question in all their minds: "All right, Steele, how the hell did you do that business with the key? You really didn't have it spotted beforehand?"

"I had no idea where it was until Thorp 'told' me," Steele answered. "It's a technique called Muscle Reading. They were doing it in the Middle Ages."

"Probably getting burned as witches too," Garrett said. "How does it work?"

"There are several books on it," I told him. "Professor Otto Dirk's is probably the best. Published in 1937. Four hundred pages. I have a copy, if you'd care to see it sometime. The technique involves reading a person's subconscious reactions by keeping a tight grip on a muscle, usually in the arm."

"It works so good that you can pull the person?"

"It works better when you pull the subject. Something about his pulling away harder in the direction he doesn't want you to go."

"You live and learn," Garrett said. "But listen, Steele, there are a couple of other things that need clearing up. For one, how did you know Thorp had made a telephone call from the Stamp Room?"

"Simple deduction, Lieutenant. He'd gone in there; he had to be doing something. What does the room offer, really, except privacy? The only lines to the switchboard open at night are those in the executive offices and the Stamp Room. You've seen the cubicle Thorp had to work in. A phone call was the only logical conclusion. He had no way of knowing that Mrs. Lorde's suspicions were directed at Schneider and not at him. With his burden of guilt, he saw accusing fingers in every gesture."

"I suppose so," Garrett said. "Which reminds me, I've got to dispatch someone to pick up Thorp's girlfriend, this Ginny Epworth; she's obviously an accessory to his embezzlement. But before I do that, suppose you give me another logical deduction: what happened to the missing stamp? Who stole it?"

"I'm sorry, Lieutenant. Despite my pose, I am not omniscient. Perhaps Thorp took it. Perhaps poor Schneider took it, for some reason we might never know. Perhaps some unknown individual took it; after all, no one has examined it closely for weeks, according to Mr. McCarthy. I doubt if it has anything to do with the murder, in any case. And I imagine it will turn up eventually."

Garrett sighed. "All right, Steele. You've been a great help, I admit it. You deserve a publicity break, so I'll see to it you get most of the credit for solving Schneider's murder. It's the least I can do."

Steele smiled—and so, of course, did I.

Two hours later—it must have been almost dawn—Steele and Ardis and I were sitting in the kitchen of his Victorian house in the Berkeley hills. I had escorted Lillian Royce to her San Francisco apartment, and then I had come across the bay to ask Steele some questions before going home myself.

My first question was: "How did you do it?"

His eyes, deceptively mild, raised from a mug of steaming coffee to meet mine over the table. "How did I do what?"

"The Hayes Two-and-a-Half-Cent Vermilion, damn it."

"Oh. Ardis—"

She tossed him one of the two rolled-up posters she had brought home with her from Lorde's—the two that had been behind the coffin inside the front window. Steele unrolled it, and his fingernail then scraped lightly at an upper corner, the mottled yellowish-red (vermilion) background to the gaudy drawing of himself. A small rectangle of paper came free, and when I leaned close I saw that two thin corner mounts of transparent plastic, the type used to mount photographs in albums, were affixed to the poster. The rectangle was a picture of President Rutherford B. Hayes.

I stared at the stamp. "You could have told me," I said.

"I don't like to worry you unnecessarily, Matthew."

"Yeah," I said. "All right—how did you get out of the coffin?"

Ardis said, "The Blue Room Illusion, or a variant of it. The coffin's lid is a double pane of glass. The bottom pane drops down at a forty-five degree angle. At the same time the lights on one side of the coffin go off, and a set on the other side come on, turning the glass into a mirror."

"Uh-huh. Then Steele disappears, and what the viewers see is—"

"—a reflected image of a photograph of Christopher pasted along the inside of the coffin, invisible from the street."

"Right," I said. "And the necessary distraction?"

"When I let that poster flap, remember? Everyone looked at me, and Christopher rolled out a hinged panel on the other side. In exactly fifteen minutes, I provided him with another distraction, and he mounted the stamp on the poster with one motion, and rolled back into the coffin. While you were having dinner, that was."

I asked Steele, "You picked the lock on the Stamp Room door?"

"Of course."

"How about the alarm?"

"I turned it off. With a duplicate key. I took an impression of the alarm lock as a customer in the Sportswear Department last week."

"One more question: you didn't figure out that Thorp had made a phone call from the Stamp Room through deduction alone, did you?"

"Not really. When I entered the room the second time, with you and everyone else, I saw immediately that the telephone had been moved. So I knew that someone had made a call in the interim—either Schneider or his killer, since McCarthy and the police had not used the instrument."

"You know," I said, "this insane passion of yours for taking on all challenges, and for creating your own when there's none around, almost got you rung in for murder this time. If your timing had been off, or if someone had spotted the stamp . . ."

"But it wasn't, and no one did," he said. "I had to solve

poor Schneider's murder to make sure I wasn't implicated in the appropriation of the Vermilion or in the homicide itself. Now *there* was a challenge."

I shook my head wearily. "You're going to return the stamp, naturally."

"Naturally. I'll arrange for it to be found somewhere in Lorde's. And its 'theft' will forever remain a mystery."

"What next, you maniac?" I asked him. "What *next?*"

"Oh, I don't know," he answered. "I've sort of been considering the crown of Henry the Seventh."

The hell of it was, I couldn't tell whether or not he was kidding . . .

Angel of Mercy

Her name was Mercy.

Born with a second name, yes, like everyone else, but it had been so long since she'd used it she could scarce remember what it was. Scarce remember so many things about her youth, long faded now—except for Father, of course. It seemed, sometimes, that she had never had a youth at all. That she'd spent her whole life on the road, first with Caleb and then with Elias, jouncing from place to place in the big black traveling wagon, always moving, drifting, never settling anywhere. Birth to death, with her small deft hands working tirelessly and her eyes asquint in smoky lamplight and her head aswirl with medicines, mixtures, measurements, what was best for this ailment, what was the proper dosage for that one. . . .

Miss Mercy. Father had been the first to call her that, in his little apothecary shop in . . . what *was* the name of the town where she'd been born? Lester? No, Dexter. Dexter, Pennsylvania. "A druggist is an angel of mercy," he said to her when she was ten or eleven. "Your name comes from my belief in that, child. Mercy. Miss Mercy. And wouldn't *you* like to be an angel of mercy one day, too?"

"Oh yes, Father, yes! Will you show me how?"

And he had shown her, with great patience, because he had no sons and because he bore no prejudice against his daughter or the daughter of any man. He had shown her carefully and well for five or six or seven years, until Mr.

President Lincoln declared war against the Confederate States of America and Father went away to bring his mercy to sick and wounded Union soldiers on far-off battlefields. But there was no mercy for him. On one of those battlefields, a place called Antietam, he was himself mortally wounded by cannon fire.

As soon as she received word of his death, she knew what she must do. She had no siblings, and Mother had died years before; Father's legacy was all that was left. And it seemed as though the next thing she knew, she was sitting on the high seat of the big black traveling wagon, alone in the beginning, then with Caleb and then Elias to drive the team of horses, bringing *her* mercy to those in need. Death to birth, birth to death—it was her true calling. Father would have been proud. He would have understood and he would have been so proud.

Miss Mercy. If it had been necessary to paint a name on the side of the wagon, that was the name she would have chosen. Just that and nothing more. It was what Caleb had called her, too, from their very first meeting in . . . Saint Louis, hadn't it been? Young and strong and restless—there driving the wagon one day, gone the next and never seen again. And Miss Mercy was the only name Elias wrote on his pad of white paper when the need arose, the name he would have spoken aloud if he hadn't been born deaf and dumb. She had chanced upon him down South somewhere. Georgia, perhaps—he was an emancipated slave from the state of Georgia. Chanced upon him, befriended him, and they had been together ever since. Twenty years? Thirty? Dear Elias. She couldn't have traveled so long and so far, or done so much, if it were not for him.

In all the long years, how many miles had they traveled together? Countless number. North and east in the spring and summer, south and west in the fall and winter. Ohio, Illinois, Minnesota, Iowa, Montana, Kansas, Nebraska, Missouri, Oklahoma, Texas . . . maybe all the states and territories there were. Civilization and wilderness frontier. Ranches, farms, settlements. Towns that had no druggist, towns that had druggists with short supplies or too little understanding of their craft. Cities, now and then, to replenish medicines that could not be gotten elsewhere. Saint Louis and . . . Chicago? Yes, Chicago. Oh, she could scarce remember them all.

And everywhere they went, the people came. The needy people with their aches and pains, ills and ailments, troubles and sorrows. First to marvel at her skill with mortar and pestle and her vast pharmacopoeial knowledge; at the cabinets and tight-fitted shelves Elias had built to hold the myriad glass bottles filled with liquids in all the colors of the rainbow, and below the shelves the rows upon rows of drawers containing ground and powdered drugs, herbs and barks, pastilles and pills. And then to buy what they needed: cough syrups, liniments, worm cures, liver medicines, stomach bitters, blood purifiers. And so much more: two-grain quinine tablets, Bateman's drops, castor oil, Epsom salts and rochelle salts and siedlitz powders, paregorics and rheumatism tonics, bottles of Lydia E. Pinkham's Vegetable Compound and Ford's Laxative Compound and Dr. Williams' Pink Pills for Pale People. And, too, in private, with their hands and eyes nervous and their voices low, embarrassed, sometimes ashamed: potency elixirs and aphrodisiacs, emmenagogues and contraceptives, Apiol Compound for suppressed and painful menstruation, fluid extract of kava-kava or emulsion of copaiba for gonorrhea, blue ointment for crab lice.

Mostly they came during the daylight hours, but now and

then someone would come rapping on the wagon's door after nightfall. And once in a long while, in the deep, dark lonesome night—

"Oh, Miss Mercy, I need help. Can you find it in your heart to help me?"

"What is your trouble, my dear?"

"I've been a fool, such a fool. A man . . . I was too friendly with him and now I'm caught."

"You're certain you're with child?"

"Oh yes. There's no mistake."

"He won't marry you?"

"He can't. He's already married. Oh, I'm such a fool. Please, will you help me?"

"There, now, you mustn't cry. I'll help you."

"You'll give me something? Truly?"

"Truly."

"Apiol Compound? I've heard that it's rich enough in mucilage to bring on—"

"No, not that. Something more certain."

"Oh, Miss Mercy, you're true to your name. You're an angel of mercy."

And again, as always, she and Elias would be back on roads good and bad, empty and well traveled. Another town, another state—here, there, no pattern to their travels, going wherever the roads took them. Never lingering anywhere for more than a day or two, except when storm or flood or accident (and once, an Indian attack) stranded them. And as always the people would come, first to marvel and then to buy: morphine, digitalis, belladonna in carefully measured doses, Dover's powder, petroleum jelly, spirits of camphor and spirits of ammonia, bone liniment and witch hazel, citrate of magnesia, blackberry balsam, oil of sassafras, throat lozenges and eye demulcents, pile remedies and asthma cures, compounds for ailments of kidney and bladder and digestive tract.

And then again, in one of their stopping places, in the deep dark lonesome night—

"Miss Mercy, you don't know what your kindness means to me."

"I do know, child. I do."

"Such a burden, such an awful burden—"

"Yes, but yours will soon be lifted."

"Just one bottle of this liquid will see to that?"

"Just one. Then you'll have no more to fear."

"It smells so sweet. What does it contain?"

"Dried sclerotia of ergot, bark of slippery elm, apiol, and gum arabic."

"Will it taste bad?"

"No, my dear. I've mixed it with syrup."

"And I'm to take the whole bottle at once?"

"Yes. But only at the time of month I tell you. And then you must immediately dispose of the bottle where no one can ever find it. Will you promise?"

"Yes, Miss Mercy. Oh yes."

"And you must tell no one I helped you. Not even your dearest friend. Will you promise?"

"I promise. I'll never tell a soul, not a living soul."

And again, as always, she and Elias would be away at the break of dawn, when dew lay soft on the grasses and mist coated the land. And sitting beside him on the high seat, remembering the poor girl who had come in the night, she would ask herself once more, as she had so many times, what Father would have said if he'd known of the mixture of ergot and slippery elm, apiol and gum arabic. Would he still think of her as an angel of mercy? Or would he hate her for betraying a sacred trust? And the answer would be as it always was: No, he could never hate her; she must have no real doubt of that. He would understand that her only aim was to bring peace to those poor foolish girls. Peace and succor in their time of need. He would understand.

And she would stop fretting then, reassured of Father's absent pride, and soon that day would end and a new one would be born. And there would be new roads, new settlements and towns, new needs to serve—so many needs to serve.

And one day she saw that it was fall again, the leaves turning crimson and gold—time to turn south and west. But first there was another town, a little town with a name like many others, in a state that might have been Kansas or perhaps Nebraska. And late that night, as Miss Mercy sat weary but strong at her mixing table, her hands busy with mortar and pestle while the lamplight flickered bright, a rapping came soft and urgent on the wagon's door.

Her name was Verity.

Names and faces meant little to Miss Mercy; there were too many to remember even for a minute. But this girl was different somehow. The name lingered, and so she knew would the face. Thin, not pretty, pale hair peeking out from under her bonnet—older than most of the ones who came alone in the night. Older, sadder, but no wiser.

Miss Mercy invited her in, invited her to sit. Verity perched primly on the stool, hands together in her lap, mouth tight-pinched at the corners. She showed no nervousness, no fear or embarrassment. Determined was the word that came to Miss Mercy's mind.

Without preamble Verity said, "I understand you're willing to help girls in trouble."

"What sort of trouble, my dear?"

"The sort that comes to foolish and unmarried girls."

"You're with child?"

Verity nodded. "I come from Riverbrook, Iowa. Do you recall the town, Miss Mercy?"

"Riverbrook? Iowa? There are so many places . . ."

"You were there four months ago. In June. The second week of June."

"The second week of June. Well. If you say I was, my dear, then of course I was."

"A girl named Grace came to see you then. Grace Potter. Do you remember her?"

"So many come to me," Miss Mercy said. "My memory isn't what it once was . . ."

"So many girls in trouble, you mean?"

"Sometimes. In the night, as you've come."

"And as Grace came."

"If you say so. As Grace came."

"You gave her something to abort her fetus. I'd like you to give me the same . . . medicine."

"If I do, will you promise to take it only at the time of month I tell you?"

"Yes."

"Will you promise to dispose of the bottle immediately after ingestion, where no one can ever find it?"

"Yes."

"And will you promise to tell no one that I helped you? Not even your dearest friend?"

"Yes."

"Then you shall have what you need."

Miss Mercy picked up her lamp, carried it to one of Elias's cabinets. When she handed the small brown unlabeled bottle to Verity, the girl removed its cork and sniffed the neck. Then Verity poured a drop onto her finger, touched her tongue to it.

"It tastes odd," she said.

"No odder than sweetened castor oil. I've mixed the compound with cherry syrup."

"Compound. What sort of compound?"

"Dried sclerotia of ergot, bark of slippery elm, apiol—"

"My God! All those blended together?"

"Yes, my dear. Why do you look so shocked?"

"Ergot contracts the womb, tightens it even more. So do dried slippery elm and apiol. All mixed together and taken in a large dose at the wrong time of month . . . cramps, paralysis, death in agony. This liquid is pure poison to a pregnant woman!"

"No, you mustn't think that—"

"I do think it," Verity said, "because it's true." She had risen to her feet and was pointing a tremulous finger at Miss Mercy. "I've studied medicine. I work in Riverbrook as a nurse and midwife."

"Nurse? Midwife? But then—"

"Then I'm not with child? No, Miss Mercy, I'm not. The truth is, I have been three months searching for you, ever since I discovered a bottle exactly like this one that Grace Potter failed to dispose of. I thought you guilty of no more than deadly quackery before tonight, but now I know different. You deliberately murdered my sister."

"Murdered?" Now it was Miss Mercy who was shocked. "Oh no, my dear. No. I brought her mercy."

"You brought her death!"

"Mercy. Your sister, all of them—only mercy."

"All of them? How many others besides Grace?"

"Does the number truly matter?"

"Does it truly—! How many, Miss Mercy?"

"I can't say. So many miles, so many places . . ."

"How many?"

"Thirty? Forty? Fifty? I can scarce remember them all . . ."

"Dear sweet Lord! You poisoned as many as *fifty* pregnant girls?"

"Unmarried girls. Poor foolish girls," Miss Mercy said gently. "There are worse things than death, oh much worse."

"What could be worse than suffering the tortures of hell before the soul is finally released?"

"Enduring the tortures of hell for years, decades, a lifetime. Isn't a few hours of pain and then peace, eternal peace, preferable to lasting torment?"

"How can you believe that bearing a child out of wedlock is so wicked—?"

"No," Miss Mercy said, "the lasting torment is in knowing, seeing the child they've brought into the world. Bastard child, child of sin. Don't you see? God punishes the unwed mother. The wages of sin is death, but God's vengeance on the living is far more terrible. I saved your sister from that. I brought her and all the others mercy from *that*."

Again she picked up the lamp. With a key from around her neck she unlocked the small satin-lined cabinet Elias had made, lifted out its contents. This she set on the table, the flickering oil lamp close beside it.

Verity looked, and cried out, and tore her gaze away.

Lamplight shone on the glass jar and on the thick formaldehyde that filled it; made a glowing chimera of the tiny twisted thing floating there, with its face that did not seem quite human, with its appendage that might have been an arm and the other that might have been a leg, with its single blind staring eye.

"Now do you understand?" Miss Mercy said. "This is my son, mine and Caleb's. God's vengeance—my poor little bastard son."

And she lifted the jar in both hands and held it tight to her bosom, cradled it and began to rock it to and fro, crooning to the fetus inside—a sweet, sad lullaby that sent Verity fleeing from the wagon, away into the deep dark lonesome night.

Connoisseur

Norman Tolliver was a connoisseur of many things: art, music, literature, gourmet cuisine, sports cars, beautiful women. But above all else, he was a connoisseur of fine wine.

Nothing gave him quite so much pleasure as the bouquet and delicate taste of a claret from the Médoc region of Bordeaux—a 1924 Mouton-Rothschild, perhaps, or a 1929 Haut-Brion; or a brilliant Burgundy such as a Clos de Vougeot 1915. His memory was still vivid of the night in Paris when an acquaintance of his father's had presented him with a glass of the *impériale* claret, the 1878 Latour Pauillac. It was Norman's opinion that a man could experience no greater moment of ecstasy than his first sip of that venerable Latour.

Norman resided in an elegant penthouse in New York that commanded a view of the city best described as lordly. That is, he resided there for six months of the year; the remaining six months were divided among Europe and the pleasure islands of the Caribbean and the Mediterranean. During his travels he expended an appreciable amount of time and money in seeking out new varieties and rare vintages of wine, most of which he arranged to have shipped to New York for placement in his private cellar.

It was his custom every Friday evening, no matter where he might happen to be, to sample an exceptional bottle of claret or Burgundy. (He enjoyed fine whites, of course—the French Sauterne, the German Moselle—but his palate and his temperament were more suited to the classic reds.) These weekly indulgences were always of a solitary nature; as a connoisseur he found the communion between man and great wine too intimate to share with anyone, too poignant to be blunted by even polite conversation.

On this particular Friday Norman happened to be in New York and the wine he happened to select was a reputedly splendid claret: the Chateau Margaux 1900. It had been given to him by a man named Roger Hume, whom Norman rather detested. Whereas he himself was the fourth-generation progeny in a family of wealth and breeding, Hume was *nouveau riche*—a large graceless individual who had compiled an overnight fortune in textiles or some such and who had retired at the age of 40 to, as he put it in his vulgar way, "find out how the upper crust lives."

Norman found the man to be boorish, dull-witted, and incredibly ignorant concerning any number of matters, including an understanding and appreciation of wine. Nevertheless, Hume had presented him with the Margaux—on the day after a small social gathering that they had both attended and at which Norman chanced to mention that he had never had the pleasure of tasting that difficult-to-obtain vintage. The man's generosity was crassly motivated, to be sure, designed only to impress; but that could be overlooked and even forgiven. A bottle of Margaux 1900 was too fine a prize to be received with any feeling other than gratitude.

At three o'clock Norman drew his study drapes against the afternoon sun and placed one of Chopin's nocturnes on his quadraphonic record changer. Then, with a keen sense of anticipation, he carefully removed the Margaux's cork and prepared to decant the wine so that it could breathe. It was his considered judgment that an aged claret should be allowed no less than five hours of contact with new air and no more than six. A healthy, living wine must be given time to breathe in order for it to express its character, release its bouquet, become *more* alive; but too much breathing causes a dulling of its subtle edge.

He lighted the candle that he had set on the Duncan Phyfe table, waited until the flame was steady, then began to slowly pour the Margaux, holding the shoulder of the bottle just above the light so that he could observe the flow of the wine as it passed through the neck. There was very little age-crust or sediment. The color, however, did not look quite right; it had a faint cloudiness, a pale brown tinge, as wine does when it has grown old too quickly.

Norman felt a sharp twinge of apprehension. He raised the decanter and sniffed the bouquet. Not good, not good at all. He swirled the wine lightly to let air mix with it and sniffed again. Oh Lord—a definite taint of sourness.

He poured a small amount into a crystal glass, prepared himself, and took a sip. Let the wine flood over and under his tongue, around his gums. And then spat the mouthful back into the glass.

The Margaux was dead.

Sour, unpalatable—*dead.*

White-faced, Norman sank onto a chair. His first feelings were of sorrow and despair, but these soon gave way to a sense of outrage focused on Roger Hume. It was Hume who had given him not a living, breathing 1900 Margaux but a desiccated *corpse;* it was Hume who had tantalized him and then left him unfulfilled, Hume who had caused him this pain and anguish, Hume who might even have been responsible for the death of the Margaux through careless mishandling. Damn the man. Damn him!

The more Norman thought about Roger Hume, the more enraged he became. Heat rose in his cheeks until they flamed scarlet. Minutes passed before he remembered his high blood pressure and his doctor's warning about undue stress; he made a conscious effort to calm himself.

When he had his emotions under control he stood, went to the telephone, found a listing for Hume in the Manhattan directory, and dialed the number. Hume's loud coarse voice answered on the third ring.

"This is Norman Tolliver, Hume," Norman said.

"Well, Norm, it's been awhile. What's the good word?"

Norm. A muscle fluttered on Norman's cheek. "If you plan to be in this afternoon, I would like a word with you."

"Oh? Something up?"

"I prefer not to discuss it on the telephone."

"Suit yourself," Hume said. "Sure, come on over. Give me a chance to show off my digs to you." He paused. "You shoot pool, by any chance?"

"No, I do not 'shoot pool.' "

"Too bad. Got a new table and I've been practicing. Hell of a good game, Norm, you should try it."

The man was a bloody Philistine. Norman said, "I'll be by directly," and cradled the handset with considerable force.

He recorked the bottle of dead Margaux and wrapped it in a towel. After which he blew out the candle, switched off his quadraphonic unit, and took the penthouse elevator to the street. Fifteen minutes later a taxi delivered him to the East Side block on which Hume's town house was situated.

Hume admitted him, allowed as how it was good to see him again, swatted him on the back (Norman shuddered and ground his teeth), and ushered him into a spacious living room. There were shelves filled with rare first editions, walls adorned with originals by Degas and Monet and Sisley, fine Kerman Orientals on the floor. But all of these works of art, Norman thought, could mean nothing to Hume; they would merely be possessions, visible evidence of his wealth. He had certainly never read any of the books or spent a moment appreciating any of the paintings. And there were cigarette burns (Norman ground his teeth again) in one of the Kerman carpets.

Hume himself was fifty pounds overweight and such a plebeian type that he looked out of place in these genteel surroundings. He wore expensive but ill-fitting clothes, much too heavy for the season because of a professed hypersensitivity to cold; his glasses were rimmed in gold-and-onyx and quite thick because of a professed astigmatism in one eye; he carried an English walking stick because of a slight limp that was the professed result of a sports car accident. He pretended to be an eccentric, but did not have the breeding, intelligence, or flair to manage even the pose of eccentricity. Looking at him now, Norman revised his previous estimate: The man was not a Philistine; he was a Neanderthal.

"How about a drink, Norm?"

"This is not a social call," Norman said.

"No?" Hume peered at him. "So what can I do for you?"

Norman unwrapped the bottle of Margaux and extended it accusingly. "*This* is what you can do for me, as you put it."

"I don't get it," Hume said.

"You gave me this Margaux last month. I trust you remember the occasion."

"Sure, I remember. But I still don't see the point—"

"The point, Hume, is that it's dead."

"Huh?"

"The wine is undrinkable. It's *dead,* Hume."

Hume threw back his head and made a sound like the braying of a jackass. "You hand me a laugh sometimes, Norm," he said, "you really do. The way you talk about wine, like it was alive or human or something."

Norman's hands had begun to tremble. "The Margaux

was alive. Now it is nothing but 79-year-old vinegar!"

"So what?" Hume said.

"So what?" A reddish haze seemed to be forming behind Norman's eyes. "So what! You insensitive idiot, don't you have any conception of what a tragedy this is?"

"Hey," Hume said, "who you calling an idiot?"

"You, you idiot. If you have another Margaux 1900, I demand it in replacement. I demand a *living* wine."

"I don't give a damn what you demand," Hume said. He was miffed too, now. "You got no right to call me an idiot, Norm; I won't stand for it. Suppose you just get on out of my house. And take your lousy bottle of wine with you."

"*My* lousy bottle of wine?" Norman said through the reddish haze. "Oh no, Hume, it's *your* lousy bottle of wine and I'm going to let *you* have it!"

Then he did exactly that: he let Hume have it. On top of the head with all his strength.

There were several confused moments that Norman could not recall afterward. When the reddish haze dissipated he discovered that all of his anger had drained away, leaving him flushed and shaken. He also discovered Hume lying quite messily dead on the cigarette-scarred Kerman, the unbroken bottle of Margaux beside him.

It was not in Norman's nature to panic in a crisis. He marshaled his emotions instead and forced himself to approach the problem at hand with cold logic.

Hume was as dead as the Margaux; there was nothing to be done about that. He could, of course, telephone the police and claim self-defense. But there was no guarantee that he would be believed, considering that this was Hume's house, and in any case he had an old-fashioned gentleman's abhorrence of adverse and sensational publicity. No, reporting Hume's demise was out of the question.

Which left the reasonable alternative of removing all traces of his presence and stealing away as if he had never come. It was unlikely that anyone had seen him entering; if he was careful his departure would be unobserved as well. And even if someone *did* happen to notice him in a casual way, he was not known in this neighborhood and there was nothing about his physical appearance that would remain fixed in a person's memory. An added point in his favor was that Hume had few friends and by self-admission preferred his own company. The body, therefore, might well go undiscovered for several days.

Norman used the towel to wipe the unbloodied surfaces of the Margaux bottle—a distasteful but necessary task—and left the bottle where it lay beside the body. Had he touched anything in the house that might also retain a fingerprint? He was certain he had not. He *had* pressed the doorbell button on the porch outside, but it would be simple enough to brush that clean before leaving. Was there anything else, anything he might have overlooked? He concluded that there wasn't.

With the towel folded inside his coat pocket, he went down the hallway to the front door. There was a magnifying-glass peephole in the center of it; he put his eye to the glass and peered out. Damn. Two women were standing on the street in front, conversing in the amiable and animated fashion of neighbors. They might decide to part company in ten seconds, but they might also decide to remain there for ten minutes.

Norman debated the advisability of exiting through the rear. But a man slipping out the back door of someone's house was much more likely to be seen and remembered than a man who departed the front. And there was still the matter of the doorbell button to be dealt with. His only intelligent choice was to wait for the street in front to become clear.

As he stood there he found himself thinking again of the tragedy of the Margaux 1900 (a far greater tragedy to his connoisseur's mind than the unlamented death of Roger Hume). It was considered by many experts to be one of the most superlative vintages in history; and the fact remained that he had yet to taste it. To have come so close and then to be denied as he had was intolerable.

It occurred to him again that perhaps Hume *did* have another bottle on the premises. While presenting the first bottle last month Hume had boasted that he maintained a "pretty well-stocked" wine cellar, though he confided that he had never had "much of a taste for the grape" and seldom availed himself of its contents. Neanderthal, indeed. But a Neanderthal with a good deal of money who had managed, through luck or wise advice, to obtain at least one bottle of an uncommon and classic wine—

Was there another Margaux 1900 in his blasted cellar?

Norman debated a second time. On the one hand it would behoove him to make as rapid an escape as possible from the scene of his impulsive crime; but on the other hand the 1900 Margaux was virtually impossible to find today, and if he passed up this opportunity to secure a bottle for himself he might never taste it. It would be a decision he might well rue for the rest of his days.

He looked once more through the peephole; the two women were still talking together outside. Which only served to cement a decision already made. He was, first and foremost, a connoisseur: he simply *had* to know if Hume had another bottle of the Margaux.

Norman located the wine cellar without difficulty. It was off the kitchen, with access through a door and down a short flight of steps. It was also adequate, he noticed in a distracted way as he descended—a smallish single room, walled and floored in concrete, containing several storage bins filled with at least two hundred bottles of wine.

But no, not just wine; remarkably *fine* wine. Reds from Châteaux Lafite, Haut-Brion, Lascombes, Cos D'Estournel, Mouton-D'Amailhacq, La Tâche, Romanée Saint-Vivant; whites from the Bommes and Barsac communes of France, from the Rhine Hessen of Germany, from Alsace and Italy and the Napa Valley of California. Norman resisted the impulse to stop and more closely examine each of the labels. He had no time to search out anything except the Margaux 1900.

He found two different Chateau Margaux clarets in the last row of bins, but neither of them was the 1900 vintage. Then, when he was about to abandon hope, he knelt in front of the final section of bins and there they were, a pair of dusty bottles whose labels matched that on the spoiled bottle upstairs.

Norman expelled a breath and removed one of them with care. Should he take the second as well? Yes: if he left it here there was no telling into whose unappreciative hands it might fall. There would doubtless be a paper sack in the kitchen in which to carry both. He withdrew the second bottle, straightened, and started to the stairs.

The door at the top was closed. Blinking, Norman paused. He could not recall having shut the door; in fact he was quite certain he had left it standing wide open. He frowned, went up the steps, set the two living Margaux 1900s down carefully at his feet, and rotated the knob.

It was locked.

It took a moment of futile shaking and rattling before he realized that the top of the door was outfitted with one of those silent pneumatic door closers. He stared at it in disbelief. Only an idiot would put such a device on the door to a wine cellar! But that was, of course, what Hume had been.

For whatever incredible reason he had had the thing installed—and it seemed obvious now that he carried on his person the key to the door latch.

There was no other way out of the cellar, no second door and no window; Norman determined that with a single sweep of his gaze. And the door looked to be fashioned of heavy solid wood, which made the task of forcing it or battering it down an insurmountable one.

He was trapped.

The irony was as bitter as the taste of the dead Margaux: trapped in Roger Hume's wine cellar with the man's murdered corpse in the living room upstairs. He had been a fool to come down here, a fool to have listened to the connoisseur in him. He could have been on his way home to his penthouse by now. Instead, here he was, locked away awaiting the eventual arrival of the police . . .

As he had done earlier, Norman made an effort to gather his wits. Perhaps all was *not* lost, despite the circumstances. He could claim to have been visiting Hume when two burly masked men entered the house; and he could claim that these men had locked him in the cellar and taken Hume away to an unknown fate. Yes, that was plausible. After all, he was a respected and influential man. Why shouldn't he be believed?

Norman began to feel a bit better. There remained the problem of survival until Hume's body was found; but as long as that did not take more than a week—an unlikely prospect—the problem was not really a serious one. He was surrounded by scores of bottles of vintage wine, and there was a certain amount of nourishment to be had from the product of the vintner's art. At least enough to keep him alive and in passable health.

Meanwhile, he would have to find ways to keep himself and his mind occupied. He could begin, he thought, by examining and making a mental catalogue of Hume's collection of vintages and varieties.

He turned from the door and surveyed the cellar again. And for the first time, something struck him as vaguely odd about it. He had not noticed it before in his haste and purpose, but now that he was locked in here with nothing to distract him—

A faint sound reached his ears and made him scowl. He could not quite identify it or its source at first; he descended the stairs again and stood at the bottom, listening. It seemed to be coming from both sides of the cellar. Norman moved to his left—and when the sound became clear the hackles rose on the back of his neck.

What it was was a soft hissing.

Roger Hume's body was discovered three days later by his twice-weekly cleaning lady. But when the police arrived at her summons, it was not Hume's death which interested them quite so much as that of the second man, whose corpse was found during a routine search of the premises.

This second "victim" lay on the floor of the wine cellar, amid a rather astonishing carnage of broken wine bottles and spilled wine. His wallet identified him as Norman Tolliver, whose name and standing were recognized by the cleaning lady, if not by the homicide detectives. The assistant medical examiner determined probable cause of death to be an apoplectic seizure, a fact which only added to the consternation of the police. Why was Tolliver locked inside Roger Hume's wine cellar? Why had he evidently smashed dozens of bottles of expensive wine? Why was he dead of natural causes and Hume dead of foul play?

They were, in a word, baffled.

One other puzzling aspect came to their attention. A plain

clothes officer noticed the faint hissing sound and verified it as forced air coming through a pair of wall ducts; he mentioned this to his lieutenant, saying that it seemed odd for a wine cellar to have heater vents like the rest of the rooms in the house. Neither detective bothered to pursue the matter, however. It struck them as unrelated to the deaths of the two men.

But it was, of course, the exact opposite: it was the key to everything. Along with several facts of which they were not yet aware: Norman's passion for wine and his high blood pressure, Roger Hume's ignorance in the finer arts and *his* hypersensitivity to cold—and the tragic effect on certain wines caused by exposure to temperatures above 60 degrees Fahrenheit.

No wonder Norman, poor fellow, suffered an apoplectic seizure. Can there be any greater horror for the true connoisseur than to find himself trapped in a cellar full of rare, aged, and irreplaceable wines that have been stupidly turned to vinegar?

Mrs. Rakubian

Three days after she murdered him with a hatchet and put his body down the dry well, Mrs. Rakubian's husband showed up alive and kicking on the front porch.

It was a hot day and Mrs. Rakubian had been in the kitchen mixing some lemonade. She mixed it tart, real tart, because Charlie always liked it sweet and made her put too much sugar in it. That was one of the reasons she'd killed him—one of three or four hundred. It wasn't the one that made her pick up the hatchet, though. That one was him blowing his nose on the front of his bib overalls. When he done that again, even after she warned him, she went and got the hatchet and give him half a dozen licks and that was that. Except for fetching the wheelbarrow and carting him off to the dry well, but that was one chore she hadn't minded at all.

Things had been mighty peaceful ever since. So peaceful that she'd taken to humming a little ditty to herself while she worked. She was humming it when she carried the tart lemonade out to the front porch. But she stopped humming it when she saw Charlie sitting there in the shade of the cottonwood tree, wiping his sweaty face with his handkerchief.

"Morning, Maude," he said. "Made some fresh lemonade, I see."

Mrs. Rakubian stared at him goggle-eyed for a few seconds. There wasn't a mark on him, not a mark!

"Something wrong, Maude?"

Mrs. Rakubian didn't answer. She put the lemonade down

on the porch table, went into the house, took the varmint gun off the rack, walked back out to the porch, and let Charlie have it with both barrels. Then she fetched the wheelbarrow and trundled what was left of him to the dry well.

"You stay dead this time, Charlie Rakubian," she said after she'd dumped him again. "Thirty years of you haunting me alive was bad enough. Don't you dare keep coming back to haunt me dead too. This time you stay put."

But Charlie didn't stay put. He was back again the next morning, all smiley and chipper, like butter wouldn't melt in his mouth and the hatchet and varmint gun hadn't durned near taken his head off twice.

Mrs. Rakubian was ready for him, though. She'd decided not to take any chances and it was a good thing she had. She didn't let him say a word this time. As soon as she saw him, she took Papa's old Frontier Colt out from under her apron and shot him right between the eyes.

"Now I'm not going to tell you again, Charlie," she said when she got him to the well. "Don't come bothering me no more. You're dead three times now and you'd better start acting like it."

She had a day and a half of peace before the sheriff's car drove in through the farm gate and stopped right in front of where she was sitting under the cottonwood tree drinking tart lemonade. The driver's door opened and Charlie got out.

Mrs. Rakubian was used to his tricks by now. She stared at him in disgust.

"Maude," Charlie said, "I got some questions to ask you. Seems Ed Beemis, the mailman, and Lloyd Poole from the gas company have disappeared and they was both last seen out this way—"

She didn't let him finish. She yanked Papa's Colt out from under her apron and let fly at him. One bullet knocked him down but the other ones missed, which allowed him to crawl to safety behind the sheriff's car. Then durned if he didn't pull a gun of his own and start blasting away at *her*.

Mrs. Rakubian flung herself into the house just in the nick of time. She locked the door behind her, reloaded Papa's Colt, and took the varmint gun down and made sure it was loaded too. Then she waited.

For a time there wasn't much noise out in the yard. Then there was—a regular commotion. Cars, voices . . . why, you'd of thought it was the Fourth of July picnic out there. Pretty soon Charlie started yelling at her over some contraption that made his voice real loud, only she didn't pay much attention to what he was saying. Instead she yelled right back at him.

"You Charlie, you go back into the well where you belong! Go on, git, and leave me be!"

Charlie didn't git and leave her be—not that she'd expected he would, after all the times he'd come back from the dead to devil her. So she was ready for him again with Papa's Colt and the varmint gun when he busted down the door and come in after her.

She *thought* she was ready, anyhow. In fact she wasn't, not with just six bullets and two loads of buckshot. Mrs. Rakubian took one look at what come piling through the door, screamed once, and swooned on the spot.

It was Charlie, all right.

But the sneaky old booger had brought a dozen other dead Charlies along with him.

Smuggler's Island

The first I heard that somebody had bought Smuggler's Island was late on a cold, foggy morning in May. Handy Manners and Davey and I had just brought the *Jennie Too* into the Camaroon Bay wharf, loaded with the day's limit in salmon—silvers mostly, with a few big kings—and Handy had gone inside the processing shed at Bay Fisheries to call for the tally clerk and the portable scales. I was helping Davey hoist up the hatch covers, and I was thinking that he handled himself fine on the boat and what a shame it'd be if he decided eventually that he didn't want to go into commercial fishing as his livelihood. A man likes to see his only son take up his chosen profession. But Davey was always talking about traveling around Europe, seeing some of the world, maybe finding a career he liked better than fishing. Well, he was only nineteen. Decisions don't come quick or easy at that age.

Anyhow, we were working on the hatch covers when I heard somebody call my name. I glanced up, and Pa and Abner Frawley were coming toward us from down-wharf, where the cafe was. I was a little surprised to see Pa out on a day like this; he usually stayed home with Jennie when it was overcast and windy because the fog and cold air aggravated his lumbago.

The two of them came up and stopped, Pa puffing on one of his home-carved meerschaum pipes. They were both seventy-two and long-retired—Abner from a manager's job at the cannery a mile up the coast, Pa from running the general store in the village—and they'd been cronies for at least half their lives. But that was where all resemblance between them ended. Abner was short and round and white-haired, and always had a smile and a joke for everybody. Pa, on the other hand, was tall and thin and dour; if he'd smiled any more than four times in the forty-seven years since I was born I can't remember it. Abner had come up from San Francisco during the Depression, but Pa was a second-generation native of Camaroon Bay, his father having emigrated from Ireland during the short-lived potato boom in the early 1900s. He was a good man and a decent father, which was why I'd given him a room in our house when Ma died six years ago, but I'd never felt close to him.

He said to me, "Looks like a good catch, Verne."

"Pretty good," I said. "How come you're out in this weather?"

"Abner's idea. He dragged me out of the house."

I looked at Abner. His eyes were bright, the way they always got when he had a choice bit of news or gossip to tell. He said, "Fella from Los Angeles went and bought Smuggler's Island. Can you beat that?"

"Bought it?" I said. "You mean outright?"

"Yep. Paid the county a hundred thousand cash."

"How'd you hear about it?"

"Jack Kewin, over to the real estate office."

"Who's the fellow who bought it?"

"Name's Roger Vauclain," Abner said. "Jack don't know any more about him. Did the buying through an agent."

Davey said, "Wonder what he wants with it?"

"Maybe he's got ideas of hunting treasure," Abner said and winked at him. "Maybe he heard about what's hidden in those caves."

Pa gave him a look. "Old fool," he said.

Davey grinned, and I smiled a little and turned to look to where Smuggler's Island sat wreathed in fog half a mile straight out across the choppy harbor. It wasn't much to look at, from a distance or up close. Just one big oblong chunk of eroded rock about an acre and a half in size, surrounded by a lot of little islets. It had a few stunted trees and shrubs, and a long headland where gulls built their nests, and a sheltered cove on the lee shore where you could put in a small boat. That was about all there was to it—except for those caves Abner had spoken of.

They were located near the lee cove and you could only get into them at low tide. Some said caves honeycombed the whole underbelly of the island, but those of us who'd ignored warnings from our parents as kids and gone exploring in them knew that this wasn't so. There were three caves and two of them had branches that led deep into the rock, but all of the tunnels were dead ends.

This business of treasure being hidden in one of those caves was just so much nonsense, of course—sort of a local legend that nobody took seriously. What the treasure was supposed to be was two million dollars in greenbacks that had been hidden by a rackets courier during Prohibition, when he'd been chased to the island by a team of Revenue agents. There was also supposed to be fifty cases of high-grade moonshine secreted there.

The bootlegging part of it had a good deal of truth though. This section of the northern California coast was a hotbed of illegal liquor traffic in the days of the Volstead Act, and the scene of several confrontations between smugglers and Revenue agents; half a dozen men on both sides had been killed, or had turned up missing and presumed dead. The way the bootleggers worked was to bring ships down from Canada outfitted as distilleries—big stills in their holds, bottling equipment, labels for a dozen different kinds of Canadian whiskey—and anchor them twenty-five miles offshore. Then local fishermen and imported hirelings would go out in their boats and carry the liquor to places along the shore, where trucks would be waiting to pick it up and transport it down to San Francisco or east into Nevada. Smuggler's Island was supposed to have been a short-term storage point for whiskey that couldn't be trucked out right away, which may or may not have been a true fact. At any rate, that was how the island got its name.

Just as I turned back to Pa and Abner, Handy came out of the processing shed with the tally clerk and the scales. He was a big, thick-necked man, Handy, with red hair and a temper to match; he was also one of the best mates around and knew as much about salmon trolling and diesel engines as anybody in Camaroon Bay. He'd been working for me eight years, but he wouldn't be much longer. He was saving up to buy a boat of his own and only needed another thousand or so to swing the down payment.

Abner told him right away about this Roger Vauclain buying Smuggler's Island. Handy grunted and said, "Anybody that'd want those rocks out there has to have rocks in his head."

"Who do you imagine he is?" Davey asked.

"One of those damn-fool rich people probably," Pa said. "Buy something for no good reason except that it's there and they want it."

"But why Smuggler's Island in particular?"

"Got a fancy name, that's why. Now he can say to his friends, why look here, I own a place up north called Smuggler's Island, supposed to have treasure hidden on it."

I said, "Well, whoever he is and whyever he bought it,

we'll find out eventually. Right now we've got a catch to unload."

"Sure is a puzzler though, ain't it, Verne?" Abner said.

"It is that," I admitted. "It's a puzzler, all right."

If you live in a small town or village, you know how it is when something happens that has no immediate explanation. Rumors start flying, based on few or no facts, and every time one of them is retold to somebody else it gets exaggerated. Nothing much goes on in a place like Camaroon Bay anyhow—conversation is pretty much limited to the weather and the actions of tourists and how the salmon are running or how the crabs seem to be thinning out a little more every year. So this Roger Vauclain buying Smuggler's Island got a lot more lip service paid to it than it would have someplace else.

Jack Kewin didn't find out much about Vauclain, just that he was some kind of wealthy resident of southern California. But that was enough for the speculations and the rumors to build on. During the next week I heard from different people that Vauclain was a real-estate speculator who was going to construct a small private club on the island; that he was a retired bootlegger who'd worked the coast during Prohibition and had bought the island for nostalgic reasons; that he was a front man for a movie company that was going to film a big spectacular in Camaroon Bay and blow up the island in the final scene. None of these rumors made much sense, but that didn't stop people from spreading them and half-believing in them.

Then, one night while we were eating supper Abner came knocking at the front door of our house on the hill above the village. Davey went and let him in, and he sat down at the table next to Pa. One look at him was enough to tell us that he'd come with news.

"Just been talking to Lloyd Simms," he said as Jennie poured him a cup of coffee. "Who do you reckon just made a reservation at the Camaroon Inn?"

"Who?" I asked.

"Roger Vauclain himself. Lloyd talked to him on the phone less than an hour ago, says he sounded pretty hard-nosed. Booked a single room for a week, be here on Thursday."

"Only a single room?" Jennie said. "Why, I'm disappointed, Abner. I expected he'd be traveling with an entourage." She's a practical woman and when it comes to things she considers nonsense, like all the hoopla over Vauclain and Smuggler's Island, her sense of humor sharpens into sarcasm.

"Might be others coming up later," Abner said seriously.

Davey said, "Week's a long time for a rich man to spend in a place like Camaroon Bay. I wonder what he figures to do all that time?"

"Tend to his island, probably," I said.

"Tend to it?" Pa said. "Tend to what? You can walk over the whole thing in two hours."

"Well, there's always the caves, Pa."

He snorted. "Grown man'd have to be a fool to go wandering in those caves. Tide comes in while he's inside, he'll drown for sure."

"What time's he due in on Thursday?" Davey asked Abner.

"Around noon, Lloyd says. Reckon we'll find out then what he's planning to do with the island."

"Not planning to do anything with it, I tell you," Pa said. "Just wants to own it."

"We'll see," Abner said. "We'll see."

Thursday was clear and warm, and it should have been a

good day for salmon; but maybe the run had started to peter out, because it took us until almost noon to make the limit. It was after two o'clock before we got the catch unloaded and weighed in at Bay Fisheries. Davey had some errands to run and Handy had logged enough extra time, so I took the *Jennie Too* over to the commercial slips myself and stayed aboard her to hose down the decks. When I was through with that I set about replacing the port outrigger line because it had started to weaken and we'd been having trouble with it.

I was doing that when a tall man came down the ramp from the quay and stood just off the bow, watching me. I didn't pay much attention to him; tourists stop by to rubberneck now and then, and if you encourage them they sometimes hang around so you can't get any work done. But then this fellow slapped a hand against his leg, as if he were annoyed, and called out in a loud voice, "Hey, you there. Fisherman."

I looked at him then, frowning. I'd heard that tone before: sharp, full of self-granted authority. Some city people are like that; to them, anybody who lives in a rural village is a low-class hick. I didn't like it and I let him see that in my face. "You talking to me?"

"Who else would I be talking to?"

I didn't say anything. He was in his forties, smooth looking, and dressed in white ducks and a crisp blue windbreaker. If nothing else, his eyes were enough to make you dislike him immediately; they were hard and unfriendly and said that he was used to getting his own way.

He said, "Where can I rent a boat?"

"What kind of boat? To go sport fishing?"

"No, not to go sport fishing. A small cruiser."

"There ain't any cruisers for rent here."

He made a disgusted sound, as if he'd expected that. "A

big outboard then," he said. "Something seaworthy."

"It's not a good idea to take a small boat out of the harbor," I said. "The ocean along here is pretty rough—"

"I don't want advice," he said. "I want a boat big enough to get me out to Smuggler's Island and back. Now who do I see about it?"

"Smuggler's Island?" I looked at him more closely. "Your name happen to be Roger Vauclain, by any chance?"

"That's right. You heard about me buying the island, I suppose. Along with everybody else in this place."

"News gets around," I said mildly.

"About that boat," he said.

"Talk to Ed Hawkins at Bay Marine on the wharf. He'll find something for you."

Vauclain gave me a curt nod and started to turn away.

I said, "Mind if I ask *you* a question now?"

He turned back. "What is it?"

"People don't go buying islands very often," I said, "particularly one like Smuggler's. I'd be interested to know your plans for it."

"You and every other damned person in Camaroon Bay."

I held my temper. "I was just asking. You don't have to give me an answer."

He was silent for a moment. Then he said, "What the hell, it's no secret. I've always wanted to live on an island, and that one out there is the only one around I can afford."

I stared at him. "You mean you're going to *build* on it?"

"That surprises you, does it?"

"It does," I said. "There's nothing on Smuggler's Island but rocks and a few trees and a couple of thousand nesting gulls. It's fogbound most of the time, and even when it's not the wind blows at thirty knots or better."

"I like fog and wind and ocean," Vauclain said. "I like isolation. I don't like people much. That satisfy you?"

I shrugged. "To each his own."

"Exactly," he said, and went away up the ramp.

I worked on the *Jennie Too* another hour, then I went over to the Wharf Cafe for a cup of coffee and a piece of pie. When I came inside I saw Pa, Abner, and Handy sitting at one of the copper-topped tables. I walked over to them.

They already knew that Vauclain had arrived in Camaroon Bay. Handy was saying, "Hell, he's about as friendly as a shark. I was over to Ed Hawkins's place shooting the breeze when he came in and demanded Ed get him a boat. Threw his weight around for fifteen minutes until Ed agreed to rent him his own Chris-Craft. Then he paid for the rental in cash, slammed two fifties on Ed's desk like they were singles and Ed was a beggar."

I sat down. "He's an eccentric, all right," I said. "I talked to him for a few minutes myself about an hour ago."

"Eccentric?" Abner said, and snorted. "That's just a name they give to people who never learned manners or good sense."

Pa said to me. "He tell you what he's fixing to do with Smuggler's Island, Verne?"

"He did, yep."

"Told Abner too, over to the Inn." Pa shook his head, glowering, and lighted a pipe. "Craziest damned thing I ever heard. Build a house on that mess of rock, live out there. Crazy, that's all."

"That's a fact," Handy said. "I'd give him more credit if he was planning to hunt for that bootlegger's treasure."

"Well, I'm sure not going to relish having him for a neighbor," Abner said. "Don't guess anybody else will either."

None of us disagreed with that. A man likes to be able to

get along with his neighbors, rich or poor. Getting along with Vauclain, it seemed, was going to be a chore for everybody.

In the next couple of days Vauclain didn't do much to improve his standing with the residents of Camaroon Bay. He snapped at merchants and waitresses, ignored anybody who tried to strike up a conversation with him, and complained twice to Lloyd Simms about the service at the Inn. The only good thing about him, most people were saying, was that he spent the better part of his days on Smuggler's Island—doing what, nobody knew exactly—and his nights locked in his room. Might have been he was drawing up plans there for the house he intended to build on the island.

Rumor now had it that Vauclain was an architect, one of those independents who'd built up a reputation, like Frank Lloyd Wright in the old days, and who only worked for private individuals and companies. This was probably true since it originated with Jack Kewin; he'd spent a little time with Vauclain and wasn't one to spread unfounded gossip. According to Jack, Vauclain had learned that the island was for sale more than six months ago and had been up twice before by helicopter from San Francisco to get an aerial view of it.

That was the way things stood on Sunday morning when Jennie and I left for church at 10:00. Afterward we had lunch at a place up the coast, and then, because the weather was cool but still clear, we went for a drive through the redwood country. It was almost 5:00 when we got back home.

Pa was in bed—his lumbago was bothering him, he said—and Davey was gone somewhere. I went into our bedroom to change out of my suit. While I was in there the telephone rang, and Jennie called out that it was for me.

When I picked up the receiver Lloyd Simms's voice said,

"Sorry to bother you, Verne, but if you're not busy I need a favor."

"I'm not busy, Lloyd. What is it?"

"Well, it's Roger Vauclain. He went out to the island this morning like usual, and he was supposed to be back at three to take a telephone call. Told me to make sure I was around then, the call was important—you know the way he talks. The call came in right on schedule, but Vauclain didn't. He's still not back, and the party calling him has been ringing me up every half hour, demanding I get hold of him. Something about a bid that has to be delivered first thing tomorrow morning."

"You want me to go out to the island, Lloyd?"

"If you wouldn't mind," he said. "I don't much care about Vauclain, the way he's been acting, but this caller is driving me up a wall. And it could be something's the matter with Vauclain's boat; can't get it started or something. Seems kind of funny he didn't come back when he said he would."

I hesitated. I didn't much want to take the time to go out to Smuggler's Island, but then if there was a chance Vauclain was in trouble I couldn't very well refuse to help.

"All right," I said. "I'll see what I can do."

We rang off, and I explained to Jennie where I was going and why. Then I drove down to the basin where the pleasure-boat slips were and took the tarp off Davey's sixteen-foot Sportliner inboard. I'd bought it for him on his sixteenth birthday, when I figured he was old enough to handle a small boat of his own, but I used it as much as he did. We're not so well off that we can afford to keep more than one pleasure craft.

The engine started right up for a change—usually you have to choke it several times on cool days—and I took her out of the slips and into the harbor. The sun was hidden by overcast now and the wind was up, building small whitecaps, running fogbanks in from the ocean but shredding them before they reached the shore. I followed the south jetty out past the breakwater and into open sea. The water was choppier there, the color of gunmetal, and the wind was pretty cold; I pulled the collar of my jacket up and put on my gloves to keep my hands from numbing on the wheel.

When I neared the island I swung around to the north shore and into the lee cove. Ed Hawkins's Chris-Craft was tied up there, all right, bow and stern lines made fast to outcroppings on a long, natural stone dock. I took the Sportliner in behind it, climbed out onto the bare rock, and made her fast. On my right, waves broke over and into the mouths of three caves, hissing long fans of spray. Gulls wheeled screeching above the headland; farther in, scrub oak and cypress danced like bobbers in the wind. It all made you feel as though you were standing on the edge of the world.

There was no sign of Vauclain anywhere at the cove, so I went up through a tangle of artichoke plants toward the center of the island. The area there was rocky but mostly flat, dotted with undergrowth and patches of sandy earth. I stopped beside a gnarled cypress and scanned from left to right. Nothing but emptiness. Then I walked out toward the headland, hunched over against the pull of the wind. But I didn't find him there either.

A sudden thought came to me as I started back and the hairs prickled on my neck. What if he'd gone into the caves and been trapped there when the tide began to flood? If that was what had happened, it was too late for me to do anything—but I started to run anyway, my eyes on the ground so I wouldn't trip over a bush or a rock.

I was almost back to the cove, coming at a different angle than before, when I saw him.

It was so unexpected that I pulled up short and almost lost my footing on loose rock. The pit of my stomach went hollow. He was lying on his back in a bed of artichokes, one arm flung out and the other wrapped across his chest. There was blood under his arm, and blood spread across the front of his windbreaker. One long look was all I needed to tell me he'd been shot and that he was dead.

Shock and an eerie sense of unreality kept me standing there another few seconds. My thoughts were jumbled; you don't think too clearly when you stumble on a dead man, a murdered man. And it was murder, I knew that well enough. There was no gun anywhere near the body, and no way it could have been an accident.

Then I turned, shivering, and ran down to the cove and took the Sportliner away from there at full throttle to call for the county sheriff.

Vauclain's death was the biggest event that had happened in Camaroon Bay in forty years, and Sunday night and Monday nobody talked about anything else. As soon as word got around that I was the one who'd discovered the body, the doorbell and the telephone didn't stop ringing—friends and neighbors, newspaper people, investigators. The only place I had any peace was on the *Jennie Too* Monday morning, and not much there because Davey and Handy wouldn't let the subject alone while we fished.

By late that afternoon the authorities had questioned just about everyone in the area. It didn't appear they'd found out anything though. Vauclain had been alone when he'd left for the island early Sunday; Abner had been down at the slips then and swore to the fact. A couple of tourists had rented boats from Ed Hawkins during the day, since the weather was pretty good, and a lot of locals were out in the harbor on pleasure craft. But whoever it was who had gone to Smuggler's Island after Vauclain, he hadn't been noticed.

As to a motive for the shooting, there were all sorts of wild speculations. Vauclain had wronged somebody in Los Angeles and that person had followed him here to take revenge. He'd treated a local citizen badly enough to trigger a murderous rage. He'd got in bad with organized crime and a contract had been put out on him. And the most far-fetched theory of all: He'd actually uncovered some sort of treasure on Smuggler's Island and somebody'd learned about it and killed him for it. But the simple truth was, nobody had any idea why Vauclain was murdered. If the sheriff's department had found any clues on the island or anywhere else, they weren't talking—but they weren't making any arrests either.

There was a lot of excitement, all right. Only underneath it all people were nervous and a little scared. A killer seemed to be loose in Camaroon Bay, and if he'd murdered once, who was to say he wouldn't do it again? A mystery is all well and good when it's happening someplace else, but when it's right on your doorstep you can't help but feel threatened and apprehensive.

I'd had about all the pestering I could stand by four o'clock, so I got into the car and drove up the coast to Shelter Cove. That gave me an hour's worth of freedom. But no sooner did I get back to Camaroon Bay, with the intention of going home and locking myself in my basement workshop, than a sheriff's cruiser pulled up behind me at a stop sign and its horn started honking. I sighed and pulled over to the curb.

It was Harry Swenson, one of the deputies who'd questioned me the day before, after I'd reported finding Vauclain's body. We knew each other well enough to be on a first-name basis. He said, "Verne, the sheriff asked me to talk to you again, see if there's anything you might have overlooked yesterday. You mind?"

"No, I don't mind," I said tiredly.

We went into the Inn and took a table at the back of the dining room. A couple of people stared at us, and I could see Lloyd Simms hovering around out by the front desk. I wondered how long it would be before I'd stop being the center of attention every time I went someplace in the village.

Over coffee, I repeated everything that had happened Sunday afternoon. Harry checked what I said with the notes he'd taken; then he shook his head and closed the notebook.

"Didn't really expect you to remember anything else," he said, "but we had to make sure. Truth is, Verne, we're up against it on this thing. Damnedest case I ever saw."

"Guess that means you haven't found out anything positive."

"Not much. If we could figure a motive, we might be able to get a handle on it from that. But we just can't find one."

I decided to give voice to one of my own theories. "What about robbery, Harry?" I asked. "Seems I heard Vauclain was carrying a lot of cash with him and throwing it around pretty freely."

"We thought of that first thing," he said. "No good, though. His wallet was on the body, and there was three hundred dollars in it and a couple of blank checks."

I frowned down at my coffee. "I don't like to say this, but you don't suppose it could be one of these thrill killings we're always reading about?"

"Man, I hope not. That's the worst kind of homicide there is."

We were silent for a minute or so. Then I said, "You find anything at all on the island? Any clues?"

He hesitated. "Well," he said finally, "I probably

shouldn't discuss it—but then, you're not the sort to break a confidence. We did find one thing near the body. Might not mean anything, but it's not the kind of item you'd expect to come across out there."

"What is it?"

"A cake of white beeswax," he said.

"Beeswax?"

"Right. Small cake of it. Suggest anything to you?"

"No," I said. "No, nothing."

"Not to us either. Aside from that, we haven't got a thing. Like I said, we're up against it. Unless we get a break in the next couple of days, I'm afraid the whole business will end up in the Unsolved file. That's unofficial, now."

"Sure," I said.

Harry finished his coffee. "I'd better get moving," he said. "Thanks for your time, Verne."

I nodded, and he stood up and walked out across the dining room. As soon as he was gone, Lloyd came over and wanted to know what we'd been talking about. But I'd begun to feel oddly nervous all of a sudden, and there was something tickling at the edge of my mind. I cut him off short, saying, "Let me be, will you, Lloyd? Just let me be for a minute."

When he drifted off, looking hurt, I sat there and rotated my cup on the table. Beeswax, I thought. I'd told Harry that it didn't suggest anything to me, and yet it did, vaguely. Beeswax. White beeswax . . .

It came to me then—and along with it a couple of other things, little things. I went cold all over, as if somebody had opened a window and let the wind inside the room. I told myself I was wrong, that it couldn't be. But I wasn't wrong. It made me sick inside, but I wasn't wrong.

I knew who had murdered Roger Vauclain.

★ ★ ★ ★ ★

When I came into the house I saw him sitting out on the sun deck, just sitting there motionless with his hands flat on his knees, staring out to sea. Or out to where Smuggler's Island sat, shining hard and ugly in the glare of the dying sun.

I didn't go out there right away. First I went into the other rooms to see if anybody else was home, but nobody was. Then, when I couldn't put it off any longer, I got myself ready to face it and walked onto the deck.

He glanced at me as I leaned back against the railing. I hadn't seen much of him since finding the body, or paid much attention to him when I had; but now I saw that his eyes looked different. They didn't blink. They looked at me, they looked past me, but they didn't blink.

"Why'd you do it, Pa?" I said. "Why'd you kill Vauclain?"

I don't know what I expected his reaction to be. But there wasn't any reaction. He wasn't startled, he wasn't frightened, he wasn't anything. He just looked away from me again and sat there like a man who has expected to hear such words for a long time.

I kept waiting for him to say something, to move, to blink his eyes. For one full minute and half of another, he did nothing. Then he sighed, soft and tired, and he said, "I knew somebody'd find out this time." His voice was steady, calm. "I'm sorry it had to be you, Verne."

"So am I."

"How'd you know?"

"You left a cake of white beeswax out there," I said. "Fell out of your pocket when you pulled the gun, I guess. You're just the only person around here who'd be likely to have white beeswax in his pocket, Pa, because you're the only person who hand-carves his own meerschaum pipes. Took me a time to remember that you use wax like that to seal the bowls and give them a luster finish."

He didn't say anything.

"Couple of other things too," I said. "You were in bed yesterday when Jennie and I got home. It was a clear day, no early fog, nothing to aggravate your lumbago. Unless you'd been out someplace where you weren't protected from the wind—someplace like in a boat on open water. Then there was Davey's Sportliner starting right up for me. Almost never does that on cool days unless it's been run recently, and the only person besides Davey and me who has a key is you."

He nodded. "It's usually the little things," he said. "I always figured it'd be some little thing that'd finally do it."

"Pa," I said, "why'd you kill him?"

"He had to go and buy the island. Then he had to decide to build a house on it. I couldn't let him do that. I went out there to talk to him, try to get him to change his mind. Took my revolver along, but only just in case; wasn't intending to use it. Only he wouldn't listen to me. Called me an old fool and worse, and then he give me a shove. He was dead before I knew it, seems like."

"What'd him building a house have to do with you?"

"He'd have brought men and equipment out there, wouldn't he? They'd have dug up everything, wouldn't they? They'd have sure dug up the Revenue man."

I thought he was rambling. "Pa . . ."

"You got a right to know about that too," he said. He blinked then, four times fast. "In 1929 a fella named Frank Eberle and me went to work for the bootleggers. Hauling whiskey. We'd go out maybe once a month in Frank's boat, me acting as shotgun, and we'd bring in a load of 'shine—mostly to Shelter Cove, but sometimes we'd be told to drop it off on Smuggler's for a day or two. It was easy money, and your ma and me needed it, what with you happening along;

and what the hell, Frank always said, we were only helping to give the people what they wanted.

"But then one night in 1932 it all went bust. We brought a shipment to the island and just after we started unloading it this man run out of the trees waving a gun and yelling that we were under arrest. A Revenue agent, been lying up there in ambush. Lying alone because he didn't figure to have much trouble, I reckon—and I found out later the government people had bigger fish to fry up to Shelter Cove that night.

"Soon as the agent showed himself, Frank panicked and started to run. Agent put a shot over his head, and before I could think on it I cut loose with the rifle I always carried. I killed him, Verne, I shot that man dead."

He paused, his face twisting with memory. I wanted to say something—but what was there to say?

Pa said, "Frank and me buried him on the island, under a couple of rocks on the center flat. Then we got out of there. I quit the bootleggers right away, but Frank, he kept on with it and got himself killed in a big shoot-out up by Eureka just before Repeal. I knew they were going to get me too someday. Only time kept passing and somehow it never happened, and I almost had myself believing it never would. Then this Vauclain came along. You see now why I couldn't let him build his house?"

"Pa," I said thickly, "it's been forty-five years since all that happened. All anybody'd have dug up was bones. Maybe there's something there to identify the Revenue agent, but there couldn't be anything that'd point to you."

"Yes, there could," he said. "Just like there was something this time—the beeswax and all. There'd have been something, all right, and they'd have come for me."

He stopped talking then, like a machine that had been turned off, and swiveled his head away and just sat staring again. There in the sun, I still felt cold. He believed what he'd just said; he honestly believed it.

I knew now why he'd been so dour and moody for most of my life, why he almost never smiled, why he'd never let me get close to him. And I knew something else too: I wasn't going to tell the sheriff any of this. He was my father and he was seventy-two years old, and I'd see to it that he didn't hurt anybody else. But the main reason was, if I let it happen that they really did come for him he wouldn't last a month. In an awful kind of way the only thing that'd been holding him together all these years was his certainty they *would* come someday.

Besides, it didn't matter anyway. He hadn't actually got away with anything. He hadn't committed one unpunished murder, or now two unpunished murders, because there is no such thing. There's just no such thing as the perfect crime.

I walked over and took the chair beside him, and together we sat quiet and looked out at Smuggler's Island. Only I didn't see it very well because my eyes were full of tears.

A Taste of Paradise

Jan and I met the Archersons at the Hotel Kolekole in Kailua Kona, on the first evening of our Hawaiian vacation. We'd booked four days on the Big Island, five on Maui, four on Kauai, and three and a half at Waikiki Beach on Oahu. It would mean a lot of shunting around, packing and unpacking, but it was our first and probably last visit to Hawaii and we had decided to see as many of the islands as we could. We'd saved three years for this trip—a second honeymoon we'd been promising ourselves for a long time—and we were determined to get the absolute most out of it.

Our room was small and faced inland; it was all we could afford at a luxury hotel like the Kolekole. So in order to sit and look at the ocean, we had to go down to the rocky, black-sand beach or to a roofed but open-sided lanai bar that overlooked the beach. The lanai bar was where we met Larry and Brenda Archerson. They were at the next table when we sat down for drinks before dinner, and Brenda was sipping a pale green drink in a tall glass. Jan is naturally friendly and curious and she asked Brenda what the drink was—something called an Emerald Bay, a specialty of the hotel that contained rum and creme de menthe and half a dozen other ingredients—and before long the four of us were chatting back and forth. They were about our age, and easy to talk to, and when they invited us to join them we agreed without hesitation.

It was their first trip to Hawaii too, and the same sort of

dream vacation as ours: "I've wanted to come here for thirty years," Brenda said, "ever since I first saw Elvis in *Blue Hawaii*." So we had that in common. But unlike us, they were traveling first-class. They'd spent a week in one of the most exclusive hotels on Maui, and had a suite here at the Kolekole, and would be staying in the islands for a total of five weeks. They were even going to spend a few days on Molokai, where Father Damien had founded his lepers' colony over a hundred years ago.

Larry told us all of this in an offhand, joking way—not at all flaunting the fact that they were obviously well-off. He was a tall, beefy fellow, losing his hair as I was and compensating for it with a thick brush moustache. Brenda was a big-boned blond with pretty gray eyes. They both wore loud Hawaiian shirts and flower leis, and Brenda had a pale pink flower—a hibiscus blossom, she told Jan—in her hair. It was plain that they doted on each other and plain that they were having the time of their lives. They kept exchanging grins and winks, touching hands, kissing every now and then like newlyweds. It was infectious. We weren't with them ten minutes before Jan and I found ourselves holding hands too.

They were from Milwaukee, where they were about to open a luxury catering service. "Another lifelong dream," Brenda said. Which gave us something else in common, in an indirect way. Jan and I own a small restaurant in Coeur d'Alene, Carpenter's Steakhouse, which we'd built into a fairly successful business over the past twenty years. Our daughter Lynn was managing it for us while we were in Hawaii.

We talked with the Archersons about the pros and cons of the food business and had another round of drinks which Larry insisted on paying for. When the drinks arrived he lifted his mai tai and said, "*Aloha nui kakou,* folks."

"That's an old Hawaiian toast," Brenda explained. "It means to your good health, or something like that. Larry is a magnet for Hawaiian words and phrases. I swear he'll be able to write a tourist phrasebook by the time we leave the islands."

"Maybe I will too, *kuu ipo.*"

She wrinkled her nose at him, then leaned over and nipped his ear. "*Kuu ipo* means sweetheart," she said to us.

When we finished our second round of drinks Larry asked, "You folks haven't had dinner yet, have you?"

We said we hadn't.

"Well then, why don't you join us in the Garden Court. Their mahimahi is out of this world. Our treat—what do you say?"

Jan seemed willing, so I said, "Fine with us. But let's make it Dutch treat."

"Nonsense. I invited you, that makes you our guests. No arguments, now—I never argue on an empty stomach."

The food was outstanding. So was the wine Larry selected to go with it, a rich French chardonnay. The Garden Court was open-sided like the lanai bar and the night breeze had a warm, velvety feel, heavy with the scents of hibiscus and plumeria. The moon, huge and near full, made the ocean look as though it were overlaid with a sheet of gold.

"Is this living or is this living?" Larry said over coffee and Kahlua.

"It's a taste of paradise," Jan said.

"It *is* paradise. Great place, great food, great drinks, great company. What more could anybody want?"

"Well, I can think of one thing," Brenda said with a leer.

Larry winked at me. "That's another great thing about the

tropics, Dick. It puts a new spark in your love life."

"I can use a spark," I said. "I think a couple of my plugs are shot."

Jan cracked me on the arm and we all laughed.

"So what are you folks doing tomorrow?" Larry asked. "Any plans?"

"Well, we thought we'd either drive down to the Volcanoes National Park or explore the northern part of the island."

"We're day-tripping up north ourselves—Waimea, Waipio Valley, the Kohala Coast. How about coming along with us?"

"Well . . ."

"Come on, it'll be fun. We rented a Caddy and there's plenty of room. You can both just sit back and relax and soak up the sights."

"Jan? Okay with you?"

She nodded, and Larry said, "Terrific. Let's get an early start—breakfast at seven, on the road by eight. That isn't too early for you folks? No? Good, then it's settled."

When the check came I offered again to pay half. He wouldn't hear of it. As we left the restaurant, Brenda said she felt like going dancing and Larry said that was a fine idea, how about making it a foursome? Jan and I begged off. It had been a long day, as travel days always are, and we were both ready for bed.

In our room Jan asked, "What do you think of them?"

"Likable and fun to be with," I said. "But exhausting. Where do they get all their energy?"

"I wish I knew."

"Larry's a little pushy. We'll have to make sure he doesn't talk us into anything we don't want to do." I paused. "You know, there's something odd about the way they act together.

It's more than just being on a dream vacation, having a good time, but I can't quite put my finger on it . . ."

"They're like a couple of kids with a big secret," Jan said. "They're so excited they're ready to burst."

We've been married for nearly thirty years and we often have similar impressions and perceptions. Sometimes it amazes me just how closely our minds work.

"That's it," I said. "That's it exactly."

The trip to the northern part of the island was enjoyable, if wearying. Larry and Brenda did most of the talking, Larry playing tour guide and unraveling an endless string of facts about Hawaii's history, geography, flora, and fauna. We spent a good part of the morning in the rustic little town of Waimea, in the saddle between Kohala Mountain and the towering Mauna Kea—the seat of the Parker Ranch, the largest individually owned cattle ranch in the United States. It was lunchtime when we finished rubbing elbows with Hawaiian cowboys and shopping for native crafts, and Brenda suggested we buy sandwich fixings and a bottle of wine and find someplace to have a picnic.

Larry wanted to hike out to the rim of the Waipio Valley and picnic there, but the rest of us weren't up to a long walk. So we drove up into the mountains on the Kawaihae road. When the road leveled out across a long plateau we might have been in California or the Pacific Northwest: rolling fields, cattle, thick stands of pine. In the middle of one of the wooded sections, Larry slowed and then pulled off onto the verge.

"Down there by that stream," he said. "Now that's a perfect spot for a picnic."

Brenda wasn't so sure. "You think it's safe? Looks like a lot of brush and grass to wade through . . ."

He laughed. "Don't worry, there aren't any wild animals up here to bother us."

"What about creepy-crawlies?"

"Nope. No poisonous snakes or spiders on any of the Hawaiian islands."

"You sure about that?"

"I'm sure, *kuu ipo*. The guidebooks never lie."

We had our picnic, and all through it Larry and Brenda nuzzled and necked and cast little knowing glances at each other. Once he whispered something in her ear that made her laugh raucously and say, "Oh, you're wicked!" Their behavior had seemed charming last night, but today it was making both Jan and me uncomfortable. Fifty-year-old adults who act like conspiratorial teenagers seem ludicrous after you've spent enough time in their company.

Kawaihae Bay was beautiful, and the clifftop view from Upolu Point was breathtaking. On the way back down the coast we stopped at a two-hundred-year-old temple built by King Kamehameha, and at the white-sand Hapuna Beach where Jan fed the remains of our picnic to the dozens of stray cats that lived there. It was after five when we got back to Kailua Kona.

The Archersons insisted again that we have dinner with them and wouldn't take no for an answer. So we stayed at the Kolekole long enough to change clothes and then went out to a restaurant that specialized in luau-style roast pork. And when we were finished eating, back we went to the hotel and up to their suite. They had a private terrace and it was the perfect place, Brenda said, to watch one of the glorious Hawaiian sunsets.

Larry brought out a bottle of Kahlua, and when he finished pouring drinks he raised his glass in another toast. "To our new *aikane,* Jan and Dick."

"*Aikane* means good friends," Brenda said.

Jan and I drank, but my heart wasn't in it and I could tell that hers wasn't either. The Archersons were wearing thin on both of us.

The evening was a reprise of yesterday's: not too hot, with a soft breeze carrying the scent of exotic flowers. Surfers played on the waves offshore. The sunset was spectacular, with fiery reds and oranges, but it didn't last long enough to suit me.

Brenda sighed elaborately as darkness closed down. "Almost the end of another perfect day. Time goes by so quickly out here, doesn't it, Jan?"

"Yes it does."

Larry said, "That's why you have to get the most out of each day in paradise. So what'll we do tomorrow? Head down to see the volcanoes, check out the lava flows?"

"There's a road called Chain of Craters that's wonderful," Brenda said. "It goes right out over the flows and at the end there's a place where you can actually walk on the lava. Parts of it are still *hot!*"

I said, "Yes, we've been looking forward to seeing the volcano area. But since you've already been there, I think we'll just drive down by ourselves in the morning—"

"No, no, we'll drive you down. We don't mind seeing it all again, do we, Brenda?"

"I sure don't. I'd love to see it again."

"Larry, I don't mean this to sound ungrateful, but Jan and I would really like some time to ourselves—"

"Look at that moon coming up, will you? It's as big as a Halloween pumpkin."

It was, but I couldn't enjoy it now. I tried again to say my piece, and again he interrupted me.

"Nothing like the moons we get back home in Wisconsin,"

he said. He put his arm around Brenda's shoulders and nuzzled her neck. "Is it, pet? Nothing at all like a Wisconsin moon."

She didn't answer. Surprisingly, her face scrunched up and her eyes glistened and I thought for a moment she would burst into tears.

Jan said, "Why, Brenda, what's the matter?"

"It's my fault," Larry said ruefully. "I used to call her that all the time, but since the accident . . . well, I try to remember not to but sometimes it just slips out."

"Call her what? Pet?"

He nodded. "Makes her think of her babies."

"Babies? But I thought you didn't have children."

"We don't. Brenda, honey, I'm sorry. We'll talk about something else . . ."

"No, it's all right." She dried her eyes on a Kleenex and then said to Jan and me, "My babies were Lhasa apsos. Brother and sister—Hansel and Gretel."

"Oh," Jan said, "dogs."

"Not just dogs—the sweetest, most gentle . . ." Brenda snuffled again. "I miss them terribly, even after six months."

"What happened to them?"

"They died in the fire, the poor babies. We buried them at Shady Acres. That's a nice name for a pet cemetery, don't you think? Shady Acres?"

"What kind of fire was it?"

"That's right, we didn't tell you, did we? Our house burned down six months ago. Right to the ground while we were at a party at a friend's place."

"Oh, that's *awful*. A total loss?"

"Everything we owned," Larry said. "It's a good thing we had insurance."

"How did it happen?"

"Well, the official verdict was that Mrs. Cooley fell asleep with a lighted cigarette in her hand."

I said, "Oh, so there was someone in the house besides the dogs. She woke up in time and managed to get out safely, this Mrs. Cooley?"

"No, she died too."

Jan and I looked at each other.

"Smoke inhalation, they said. The way it looked, she woke up all right and tried to get out, but the smoke got her before she could. They found her by the front door."

"Hansel and Gretel were trapped in the kitchen," Brenda said. "She was so selfish—she just tried to save herself."

Jan made a throat-clearing sound. "You sound as though you didn't like this woman very much."

"We didn't. She was an old witch."

"Then why did you let her stay in your house?"

"She paid us rent. Not much, just a pittance."

"But if you didn't like her—"

"She was my mother," Brenda said.

Far below, on the lanai bar, the hotel musicians began to play ukuleles and sing a lilting Hawaiian song. Brenda leaned forward, listening, smiling dreamily. "That's 'Maui No Ka Oi,' " she said. "One of my all-time favorites."

Larry was watching Jan and me. He said, "Mrs. Cooley really was an awful woman, no kidding. Mean, carping—and stingy as hell. She knew how much we wanted to start our catering business but she just wouldn't let us have the money. If she hadn't died in the fire . . . well, we wouldn't be here with you nice folks. Funny the way things happen sometimes, isn't it?"

Neither Jan nor I said anything. Instead we got to our feet, almost as one.

"Hey," Larry said, "you're not leaving?"

I said yes, we were leaving.

"But the night's young. I thought maybe we'd go dancing, take in one of the Polynesian revues—"

"It's been a long day."

"Sure, I understand. You folks still have some jet lag too, I'll bet. Get plenty of sleep and call us when you wake up, then we'll all go have breakfast before we head for the volcanoes."

They walked us to the door. Brenda said, "Sleep tight, you lovely people," and then we were alone in the hallway.

We didn't go to our room; instead we went to the small, quiet lobby bar for drinks we both badly needed. When the drinks came, Jan spoke for the first time since we'd left the Archersons. "My God," she said, "I had no idea they were like that—so cold and insensitive under all that bubbly charm. Crying over a pair of dogs and not even a kind word for her mother. They're actually glad the poor woman is dead."

"More than glad. And much worse than insensitive."

"What do you mean?"

"You know what I mean."

"You don't think they—"

"That's just what I think. What we both think."

"Her own mother?"

"Yes. They arranged that fire somehow so Mrs. Cooley would be caught in it, and sacrificed their dogs so it would look even more like an accident."

"For her money," Jan said slowly. "So they could start their catering business."

"Yes."

"Dick . . . we can't just ignore this. We've got to *do* something."

"What would you suggest?"

"I don't know, contact the police in Milwaukee . . ."

"And tell them what that can be proven? The Archersons didn't admit anything incriminating to us. Besides, there must have been an investigation at the time. If there'd been any evidence against them, they wouldn't have gotten Mrs. Cooley's money and they wouldn't be here celebrating."

"But that means they'll get away with it, with cold-blooded murder!"

"Jan, they already have. And they're proud of it, proud of their own cleverness. I'll tell you another thing I think. I think they contrived to tell us the story on purpose, with just enough hints so we'd figure out the truth."

"Why would they do that?"

"The same reason they latched onto us, convinced themselves we're kindred spirits. The same reason they're so damned eager. They're looking for somebody to share their secret with."

"Dear God."

We were silent after that. The tropical night was no longer soft; the air had a close, sticky feel. The smell of hibiscus and plumeria had turned cloyingly sweet. I swallowed some of my drink, and it tasted bitter. Paradise tasted bitter now, the way it must have to Adam after Eve bit into the forbidden fruit.

The guidebooks do lie, I thought. There are serpents in this Eden, too.

Early the next morning, very early, we checked out of the Kolekole and took the first interisland flight to Honolulu and then the first plane home.

Under the Skin

In the lobby lounge of the St. Francis Hotel, where he and Tom Olivet had gone for a drink after the A.C.T. dramatic production was over, Walter Carpenter sipped his second Scotch-and-water and thought that he was a pretty lucky man. Good job, happy marriage, kids of whom he could be proud, and a best friend who had a similar temperament, similar attitudes, aspirations, likes and dislikes. Most people went through life claiming lots of casual friends and a few close ones, but seldom did a perfectly compatible relationship develop as it had between Tom and him. He knew brothers who were not nearly as close. Walter smiled. That's just what the two of us are like, he thought. Brothers.

Across the table Tom said, "Why the sudden smile?"

"Oh, just thinking that we're a hell of a team," Walter said.

"Sure," Tom said. "Carpenter and Olivet, the Gold Dust Twins."

Walter laughed. "No, I mean it. Did you ever stop to think how few friends get along as well as we do? I mean, we like to do the same things, go to the same places. The play tonight, for example. I couldn't get Cynthia to go, but as soon as I mentioned it to you, you were all set for it."

"Well, we've known each other for twenty years," Tom said. "Two people spend as much time together as we have, they get to thinking alike and acting alike. I guess we're one head on just about everything, all right."

"A couple of carbon copies," Walter said. "Here's to friendship."

They raised their glasses and drank, and when Walter put his down on the table he noticed the hands on his wristwatch. "Hey," he said. "It's almost eleven-thirty. We'd better hustle if we're going to catch the train. Last one for Daly City leaves at midnight."

"Right," Tom said.

They split the check down the middle, then left the hotel and walked down Powell Street to the Bay Area Rapid Transit station at Market. Ordinarily one of them would have driven in that morning from the Monterey Heights area where they lived two blocks apart, but Tom's car was in the garage for minor repairs, and Walter's wife Cynthia had needed their car for errands. So they had ridden a BART train in, and after work they'd had dinner in a restaurant near Union Square before going on to the play.

Inside the Powell station Walter called Cynthia from a pay phone and told her they were taking the next train out; she said she would pick them up at Glen Park. Then he and Tom rode the escalator down to the train platform. Some twenty people stood or sat there waiting for trains, half a dozen of them drunks and other unsavory-looking types. Subway crime had not been much of a problem since BART, which connected several San Francisco points with a number of East Bay cities, opened two years earlier. Still, there were isolated incidents. Walter began to feel vaguely nervous; it was the first time he had gone anywhere this late by train.

The nervousness eased when a westbound pulled in almost immediately and none of the unsavory-looking types followed them into a nearly empty car. They sat together, Walter next to the window. Once the train had pulled out he could see their reflections in the window glass. Hell, he thought, the two of us even look alike sometimes. Carbon copies, for a fact. Brothers of the spirit.

A young man in workman's garb got off at the 24th and Mission stop, leaving them alone in the car. Walter's ears popped as the train picked up speed for the run to Glen Park. He said, "These new babies really move, don't they?"

"That's for sure," Tom said.

"You ever ride a fast-express passenger train?"

"No," Tom said. "You?"

"No. Say, you know what would be fun?"

"What?"

"Taking a train trip across Canada," Walter said. "They've still got crack passenger expresses up there—they run across the whole of Canada from Vancouver to Montreal."

"Yeah, I've heard about those," Tom said.

"Maybe we could take the families up there and ride one of them next summer," Walter said. "You know, fly to Vancouver and then fly home from Montreal."

"Sounds great to me."

"Think the wives would go for it?"

"I don't see why not."

For a couple of minutes the tunnel lights flashed by in a yellow blur; then the train began to slow and the globes steadied into a widening chain. When they slid out of the tunnel into the Glen Park station, Tom stood up and Walter followed him to the doors. They stepped out. No one was waiting to get on, and the doors hissed closed again almost immediately. The westbound rumbled ahead into the tunnel that led to Daly City.

The platform was empty except for a man in an overcoat and a baseball cap lounging against the tiled wall that sided the escalators; Walter and Tom had been the only passengers to get off. The nearest of the two electronic clock-and-message boards suspended above the platform read 12:02.

The sound of the train faded into silence as they walked toward the escalators, and their steps echoed hollowly. Midnight-empty this way, the fluorescent-lit station had an eerie quality. Walter felt the faint uneasiness return and impulsively quickened his pace.

They were ten yards from the escalators when the man in the overcoat moved away from the wall and came toward them. He had the collar pulled up around his face and his chin tucked down into it; the bill of the baseball cap hid his forehead, so that his features were shadowy. His right hand was inside a coat pocket.

The hair prickled on Walter's neck. He glanced at Tom to keep from staring at the approaching man, but Tom did not seem to have noticed him at all.

Just before they reached the escalators the man in the overcoat stepped across in front of them, blocking their way, and planted his feet. They pulled up short. Tom said, "Hey," and Walter thought in sudden alarm: Oh, my God!

The man took his hand out of his pocket and showed them the long thin blade of a knife. "Wallets," he said flatly. "Hurry it up, don't make me use this."

Walter's breath seemed to clog in his lungs; he tasted the brassiness of fear. There was a moment of tense inactivity, the three of them as motionless as wax statues in a museum exhibit. Then, jerkily, his hand trembling, Walter reached into his jacket pocket and fumbled his wallet out.

But Tom just stood staring, first at the knife and then at the man's shadowed face. He did not seem to be afraid. His lips were pinched instead with anger. "A damned mugger," he said.

Walter said, "Tom, for God's sake!" and extended his

wallet. The man grabbed it out of his hand, shoved it into the other slash pocket. He moved the knife slightly in front of Tom.

"Get it out," he said.

"No," Tom said, "I'll be damned if I will."

Walter knew then, instantly, what was going to happen next. Close as the two of them were, he was sensitive to Tom's moods. He opened his mouth to shout at him, tell him not to do it; he tried to make himself grab onto Tom and stop him physically. But the muscles in his body seemed paralyzed.

Then it was too late. Tom struck the man's wrist, knocked it and the knife to one side, and lunged forward.

Walter stood there, unable to move, and watched the mugger sidestep awkwardly, pulling the knife back. The coat collar fell away, the baseball cap flew off as Tom's fist grazed the side of the man's head—and Walter could see the mugger's face clearly: beard-stubbled, jutting chin, flattened nose, wild blazing eyes.

The knife, glinting light from the overhead fluorescents, flashed between the mugger and Tom, and Tom stiffened and made a grunting, gasping noise. Walter looked on in horror as the man stepped back with the knife, blood on the blade now, blood on his hand. Tom turned and clutched at his stomach, eyes glazing, and then his knees buckled and he toppled over and lay still.

He killed him, Walter thought, he killed Tom—but he did not feel anything yet. Shock had given the whole thing a terrible dreamlike aspect. The mugger turned toward him, looked at him out of those burning eyes. Walter wanted to run, but there was nowhere to go with the tracks on both sides of the platform, the electrified rails down there, and the mugger blocking the escalators. And he could not make himself move now any more than he had been able to move when he realized Tom intended to fight.

The man in the overcoat took a step toward him, and in that moment, from inside the eastbound tunnel, there was the faint rumble of an approaching train. The suspended message board flashed CONCORD, and the mugger looked up there, looked back at Walter. The eyes burned into him an instant longer, holding him transfixed. Then the man turned sharply, scooped up his baseball cap, and ran up the escalator.

Seconds later he was gone, and the train was there instead, filling the station with a rush of sound that Walter could barely hear for the thunder of his heart.

The policeman was a short thick-set man with a black mustache, and when Walter finished speaking he looked up gravely from his notebook. "And that's everything that happened, Mr. Carpenter?"

"Yes," Walter said, "that's everything."

He was sitting on one of the round tile-and-concrete benches in the center of the platform. He had been sitting there ever since it happened. When the eastbound train had braked to a halt, one of its disembarking passengers had been a BART security officer. One train too late, Walter remembered thinking dully at the time; he's one train too late. The security officer had asked a couple of terse questions, then had draped his coat over Tom and gone upstairs to call the police.

"What can you tell me about the man who did it?" the policeman asked. "Can you give me a description of him?"

Walter's eyes were wet; he took out his handkerchief and wiped them, shielding his face with the cloth, then closing his eyes behind it. When he did that he could see the face of the mugger: the stubbled cheeks, the jutting chin, the flat nose—and the eyes, above all those malignant eyes that had said as clearly as though the man had spoken the words aloud: *I've got your wallet, I know where you live. If you say anything to the cops I'll come after you and give you what I gave your friend.*

Walter shuddered, opened his eyes, lowered the handkerchief, and looked over to where the group of police and laboratory personnel were working around the body. Tom Olivet's body. Tom Olivet, lying there dead.

We were like brothers, Walter thought. We were just like brothers.

"I can't tell you anything about the mugger," he said to the policeman. "I didn't get a good look at him. I can't tell you anything at all."

Prose Bowl

(with Barry N. Malzberg)

Standing there at midfield in the Coliseum, in front of a hundred thousand screaming New-Sport fans and a TriDim audience estimated at thirty million, I felt a lot of different emotions: excitement, pride, tension, and maybe just a touch of fear. I still couldn't believe that I was here—Rex Sackett, the youngest ever to make it all the way through the playoffs to the Prose Bowl. But I'd done it, and if I cleared one more hurdle I would be the new world champion.

Just one more hurdle.

I looked across the Line at the old man. Leon Culp, better known as The Cranker. Fifty-seven years old, twenty-million words in a career spanning almost four decades. Twice defeated in the quarter-finals, once defeated in the semi-finals two years ago. His first time in the Prose Bowl too, and he was the sentimental favorite. I was just a kid, an upstart; by all rights, a lot of the scribes had been saying, I didn't deserve to be here at my age. But the odds-makers had made me a 3–2 favorite because of my youth and stamina and the way I had handled my opponents in the playoffs. And because there were also a lot of people who felt The Cranker couldn't win the big ones; that he depended too much on the Fuel now, that he was pretty near washed up and had made it this far only because of weak competition.

Maybe all of that was true, but I wasn't so sure. Leon Culp had always been my idol; I had grown up reading and studying him, and in his time and despite his misfortune in past Prose Bowl races—he was the best there was. I'd been in awe of him when I was a wet-behind-the-ears kid in the Junior Creative Leagues, and I was still a little in awe of him now.

It wasn't that I lacked confidence in myself. I had plenty of confidence, and plenty of desire too; I wanted to win not only for myself and the $100,000 championship prize, but for Sally, and for Mort Taylor, the best agent in the business, and most of all for Mom and Dad, who had supported me during those first five lean years when I was struggling in the semi-pros. Still, I couldn't seem to shake that sense of nervous wonder. This wasn't any ordinary pro I was about to go up against. This was The Cranker.

It was almost time for the Face-Off to begin. The PA announcer introduced me first, because as the youngest of the contestants I was wearing the visitor's red, and I stepped out and waved at the packed stands. There was a chorus of cheers, particularly from over in G Section where Sally and Mort and the folks were sitting with the Sackett Boosters. The band struck up my old school song; I felt my eyes dampen as I listened.

When the announcer called out The Cranker's name, the cheers were even louder—but there were a few catcalls mixed in too. He didn't seem to pay any attention either way. He just stood without moving, his seamed old face set in stoic determination. In his blue uniform tunic, outlined against the hot New Year's Day sky, he looked bigger than he really was—awesome, implacable. Unbeatable.

Everybody stood up for the National Anthem. Then there was another uproar from the fans—I'd never imagined how deafening it could get down here on the floor of the Prose Bowl—and finally the head Editor trotted out and called us over for the coin flip. I called Tails in the air, and the coin fell to the turf and came up Tails. The Head Editor moved over to me and patted my shoulders to indicate I'd won the toss; the Sackett Boosters bellowed their approval. Through all of this, Culp remained motionless and aloof, not looking at me or the Head Editor or anything else, it seemed.

We went back to the Line and got ready. I was becoming more and more tense as the Face-Off neared; the palms of my hands were slick and my head seemed empty. What if I can't think of a title? I thought. What if I can't think of an opening sentence?

"Be cool, kid," Mort Taylor had told me earlier. "Don't try to force it. The words'll come, just like they always have."

The Cranker and I stood facing each other, looking at the huge electronic scoreboards at opposite ends of the field. Then, out of the corner of my eye, I saw the Head Editor wave his red starting flag at the Line Editor; and in the next instant the two plot topics selected by the officials flashed on the board.

A. FUTURISTIC LOVE-ADVENTURE

B. MID-TWENTIETH CENTURY DETECTIVE

I had five seconds to make my choice. Both of the topics looked tough, but this was the Prose Bowl and nothing came easy in the championship. I made an arbitrary selection and yelled out "Plot B!" to the Head Editor. He unfurled his white flag with the letter B on it, and immediately the PA announcer's voice boomed, "Rex Sackett chooses Plot B!"

The crowd broke into thunderous applause; the sound of it was like a pressure against my eardrums. I could feel my pulse racing in hard irregular rhythm and my stomach was knotted up. I tried not to think about the thirty million people watching me on the TriDim close-ups.

The Line Editor's claxon went off.

The Cranker and I broke for our typewriters. And all of a sudden, as I was sliding into my chair, I felt control and a kind of calm come into me. That was the way it always was with me, the way it always was with the great ones, Mort had said: no matter how nervous you were before the start of a match, once the horn sounded your professionalism took over and you forgot everything except the job you had to do.

I had a title even before I reached for the first sheet of paper beside the typewriter, and I had the first sentence as soon as I rolled the sheet into the platen. I fired out the title—THE MICAWBER DIAMOND—jabbed down the opening sentence and the rest of the narrative hook, and was into the second paragraph before I heard Culp's machine begin its amplified hammering across the Line.

A hundred thousand voices screamed for speed and continuity. The Cranker's rooting section and the Sackett Boosters made the most noise; I knew Sally would be leading the cheers on my side, and I had a sharp mental image of her in her red-and-white sweater with the big S on the front. Sweet, wonderful Sally . . .

I hunched forward, teeth locked around the stem of my old briar, and drove through two more paragraphs of stage-setting. End of page one. I glanced up at the south-end scoreboard as I ripped the sheet out of the platen and rolled in a new one. SACKETT 226, CULP 187. I laid in half a page of flashback, working the adjectives and the adverbs to build up my count, powered through eight lines of descriptive transition, and came into the first passage of dialogue. Up on the board, what I was writing appeared in foot-high electronic printout, as if the words were emblazoned on the sky itself.

SAM SLEDGE STALKED ACROSS HIS PLUSH OFFICE, LEAVING FOOTPRINTS IN THE THICK SHAG CARPET LIKE ANGRY DOUGHNUTS. VELDA VANCE, ALLURINGLY BEAUTIFUL SECRETARY TO SLEDGE AND CHANDLER INVESTIGATIONS,

LOOKED UP IN ALARM. "SOMEBODY MURDERED MILES CHANDLER LAST NIGHT," HE GRITTED TO HER, "AND STOLE THE MICAWBER DIAMOND HE WAS GUARDING."

It was solid stuff, I knew that. Not my best, but plenty good enough and just what the fans wanted. The sound of my name echoing through the great stadium put chills on my back.

"Sackett! Hack it! Sackett, hack it! Sackett hack it Sackett hack it!"

I finished the last line on page two and had the clean sheet into the machine in two seconds flat. My eyes found the scoreboard again as I pounded the keys: SACKETT 529, CULP 430. Hundred-word lead, but that was nothing in this early going. Without losing speed or concentration, I sneaked a look at what The Cranker was punching out.

THE DENEBIAN GREEN-BEAST CAME TOWARD HER, MOVING WITH A CURIOUSLY FLOWING MOTION, ITS TENTACLES SWAYING IN A SENSUAL DANCE OF ALIEN LUST. SHE STOOD FROZEN AGAINST A RUDDER OF ROCK AND STARED AT THE THING IN HORROR. THE UNDULATING TENTACLES REACHED TOWARD HER AND THE GREEN WAVES OF DAMP WHICH THE BEAST EXUDED SENT SHUDDERS THROUGH HER.

God, I thought, that's top-line prose. He's inspired, he's pulling out all the stops.

The crowd sensed it too. I could hear his cheerleaders chanting, almost drowning out the cries from my own rooters across the way.

"Come on, Culp! Write that pulp!"

I was in the most intense struggle of my life, there was no doubt about that. I'd known it was going to be rough, but knowing it and then being in the middle of it were two different things. The Cranker was a legend in his own time; when he was right, no one had his facility, his speed, his edge with the cutting transitions, his ability to produce under stress. If he could maintain pace and narrative drive, there wasn't a writer on earth who could beat him—

SACKETT 920, CULP 874.

The score registered on my mind, and I realized with a jolt that my own pace had slacked off: Culp had cut my lead by more than half. That was what happened to you when you started worrying about your opponent and what he was doing. I could hear Mort's voice again, echoing in my memory: "The pressure will turn your head, kid, if you let it. But I don't think it will. I think you're made of the real stuff; I think you've got the guts and the heart."

THE ANGER ON MICAWBER'S FACE MELTED AWAY LIKE SOAP IN A SOAP DISH UNDER A STREAM OF HOT DIRTY WATER.

I jammed out that line and I knew I was back in the groove, beginning to crank near the top of my form. The sound of my machine climbed to a staccato pulse. Dialogue, some fast foreshadowing, a string of four adjectives that drew a burst of applause from the Sackett Boosters. I could feel my wrists starting to knot up from the strain, and there was pain in my left leg where I'd pulled a hamstring during the semi-final match against the Kansas City Flash. But I didn't pay any attention to that; I had written in pain before and I wasn't about to let it bother me now. I just kept firing out my prose.

Only I wasn't gaining back any of my lead, I saw then. The foot-high numerals read SACKETT 1163, CULP 1127. The Cranker had hit his stride too, and he was matching me word for word, sentence for sentence.

SHE HAD NO MORE STRENGTH LEFT TO RUN.

SHE WAS TRAPPED NOW, THERE WAS NO ESCAPE. A SCREAM BURST FROM HER THROAT AS THE BEAST BOUNDED UP TO HER AND DREW HER INTO ITS AWFUL CLUTCHES, BREATHING GREEN FUMES AGAINST HER FACEPLATE. IT WAS GOING TO WORK ITS WILL ON HER! IT WAS GOING TO DO UNSPEAKABLE THINGS TO HER BODY!

"Culp, Culp, Culp!"

THE NIGHT WAS DARK AND WET AND COLD AND THE RAIN FELL ON SLEDGE LIKE A MILLION TEARS FROM A MILLION LOST LOVES ON A MILLION WORLDS IN A MILLION GALAXIES.

"Sackett, Sackett, Sackett!"

Sweat streamed into my eyes, made the numerals on the board seem smeared and glistening: SACKETT 1895, CULP 1857. I ducked my head against the sleeve of my tunic and slid a new sheet into the machine. On the other side of the Line, The Cranker was sitting straight and stiff behind his typewriter, fingers flying, his shaggy head wreathed in cigarette smoke. But he wasn't just hitting the keys, he was *attacking* them—as if they, not me, were the enemy and he was trying to club them into submission.

I reached back for a little extra, raced through the rest of the transition, slammed out three paragraphs of introspection and five more of dialogue. New page. More dialogue, then another narrative hook to foreshadow the first confrontation scene. New page. Description and some cat-and-mouse action to build suspense.

AS HE WAITED IN THE DARK ALLEY FOR THE GUY WHO WAS FOLLOWING HIM, SLEDGE'S RIGHT HAND ITCHED AROUND THE GUN IN HIS POCKET. HE COULD FEEL THE OLD FAMILIAR RAGE BURNING INSIDE HIM, MAKING HIS BLOOD BOIL

LIKE WATER IN A KETTLE ON THE OLD WOOD-BURNING STOVE IN HIS OLD MAN'S FOURTH-FLOOR WALK-UP IN

My typewriter locked. I heard the cheering rise to a crescendo; two hundred thousand hands commenced clapping as the Line Editor's horn blared.

End of the first quarter.

SACKETT 2500, CULP 2473.

I leaned back in my chair, sleeving more wetness from my face, and took several deep breaths. The Cranker had got to his feet. He stood in a rigid posture, a fresh cigarette between his lips, and squinted toward the sidelines. His Seconds were already on the field, running toward him with water bucket and a container of Fuel.

My own Seconds reached me a short time later. One of them extended Fuel, but even though my mouth was dry, sandy, I shook my head and gestured him away. Mort and I had agreed that I should hold off on the Fuel as long as possible; it was part of the game plan we had worked out.

By the time I finished splashing water on my face and toweling off, there was less than a minute of the time-out left. I looked over at G Section. I couldn't pick Mom and Dad out of the sea of faces, or Sally or Mort either, but just knowing they were there was enough.

I took my place, knocked dottle out of the briar, tamped in some fresh tobacco, and fired it. My mind was already racing, working ahead—a full four sentences when Culp sat down again and the Head Editor raised the red starting flag.

Claxon.

THE OLD NEIGHBORHOOD. THE FOLLOWER HAD SOMETHING TO DO WITH HIS PARTNER'S MURDER AND THE THEFT OF THE DIAMOND,

SLEDGE WAS SURE OF THAT. HE WAS GOING TO GET SOME ANSWERS NOW, ONE WAY OR ANOTHER.

And I was off, banging my machine at the same feverish pace of the first period. I cut through a full page of action, interspersing it with dialogue, drawing it out; the scene was good for another 500 words, at least. Twelve pages down and the thirteenth in the typewriter. My quality level was still good, but when I glanced up at the board, I saw that The Cranker was once again cranking at the top of his form.

BUT EVEN WHILE SHE WAS CLINGING TO THE STARFLEET CAPTAIN WHO HAD SAVED HER LIFE, SHE FELT A STRANGE SADNESS. THE GREEN-BEAST HAD BEEN DISINTEGRATED AND WAS NOTHING MORE NOW THAN A PUDDLE OF GREEN ON THE DUSTY SANDS OF DENEB, LIKE A SPLOTCH OF PAINT ON AN ALIEN CANVAS. THE HORROR WAS OVER, AND YET . . . AND YET, DESPITE HER REVULSION, THE THING HAD STIRRED SOMETHING DEEP AND PRIMITIVE INSIDE HER THAT SHE WAS ONLY JUST BEGINNING TO UNDERSTAND.

"Culp, Culp—crank that pulp!"

My lead had dwindled to a mere twelve words: the scoreboard read SACKETT 3359, CULP 3347. The Cranker was making his move now, and he was doing it despite the fact that I was working at maximum speed.

The feeling of tension and uncertainty began to gnaw at me again. I fought it down, concentrated even more intensely, punching the keys so hard that pain shot up both wrists. Fresh sweat rolled off me; the hot sun lay on the back of my neck like a burning hand.

SLEDGE SNARLED, "YOU'LL TALK, ALL RIGHT!"

AND SWATTED THE GUY ACROSS THE HEAD WITH HIS FORTY-FIVE. THE GUY REELED AND STAGGERED INTO THE WET ALLEY WALL. SLEDGE MOVED IN, TRANSFERRING THE GUN TO HIS LEFT HAND. HE HIT THE FOLLOWER A SECOND TIME, HIT HIM IN THE MOUTH WITH A HAND LIKE A FIST

The Head Editor's whistle blew.

And my typewriter locked, jamming my fingers.

Penalty. Penalty!

My throat closed up. I snapped my head over toward the sidelines and saw the ten-second penalty flag waving the green-and-black one that meant "Phrasing Unacceptable." The crowd was making a magnified sound that was half excited, half groaning; I knew the TriDim cameras would have homed in on me for a series of closeups. I could feel my face reddening. First penalty of the match and I had let it happen to me.

But that wasn't the worst part. The worst part was that it was going to cost me the lead: The Cranker's typewriter was still clattering on at white heat, churning out words and sentences that flashed like taunts on the board.

I counted off the seconds in my mind, and when the Head Editor's flag dropped and my machine unlocked, I flailed the keys angrily, rewriting the penalty sentence: HE HIT THE FOLLOWER A SECOND TIME, HIT HIM IN THE MOUTH WITH A HAND LIKE A CEMENT BLOCK. But the damage had been done, all right. The board told me that and told everyone else too.

CULP 3899, SACKETT 3878.

The penalty seemed to have energized The Cranker, given him a psychological lift; he was working faster than ever now, with even more savagery. I felt a little wrench of fear. About the only way you could beat one of the greats was to take the lead early on and hold it. Once an experienced old pro like Culp got in front, the advantage was all his.

A quote dropped into my mind, one I'd read a long time ago in an Old-Sports history text, and it made me shiver: "Going up against the best is a little bit like going up against Death."

I had my own speed back now, but my concentration wasn't as sharp as it had been before the penalty; a couple of times I hit the wrong keys, misspelled words and then had to retype them. It was just the kind of penalty-reaction Mort had warned me against. "Penalties don't mean a thing," he'd said. "What you've got to watch out for is worrying about them, letting them dam up the flow or lead you into another mistake."

But it wasn't Mort out here in the hot Prose Bowl sun. It wasn't Mort going head-to-head against a legend . . .

The amplified sound of Culp's machine seemed louder than my own, steadier, more rhythmic. Nervously I checked the board again. His stuff was coming so fast now that it might have been written by one of the experimental prose-computers instead of a pulpeteer.

SHE LOOKED OUT THROUGH THE SHIP'S VIEWSCREEN AT THE EMPTY SWEEP OF SPACE. BEHIND HER SHE COULD HEAR THE CAPTAIN TALKING TO THE BASE COMMANDER AT EARTH COLONY SEVEN, RELAYING THE INFORMATION ABOUT THE SHUTTLE-SHIP CRASH ON DENEB. "ONLY ONE SURVIVOR," HE WAS SAYING. YES, SHE THOUGHT, ONLY ONE SURVIVOR. BUT I WISH THERE HADN'T BEEN ANY. IF I'D DIED IN THE CRASH TOO, THEN I WOULDN'T HAVE BEEN ATTACKED BY THE GREEN-BEAST. AND I

WOULDN'T BE FEELING THESE STRANGE AND TERRIBLE EMOTIONS, THIS SENSE OF UNFULFILLMENT AND DEPRIVATION.

Some of the fans were on their feet, screaming *"Cranker! Cranker!"*

CULP 4250, SACKETT 4196.

I felt light-headed, giddy with tension; but the adrenaline kept flowing and the words kept coming, pouring out of my subconscious and through the mind-haze and out into the blazing afternoon—nouns, verbs, adjectives, adverbs. Don't let him gain any more ground. Stay close. Stay close!

SLEDGE FOLLOWED THE FAT MAN THROUGH THE HEAVY DARKNESS ALONG THE RIVER. THE STENCH OF FISH AND MUD AND GARBAGE WAFTED UP FROM THE OILY BLACK WATER AND SLAPPED HIM ACROSS THE FACE LIKE A DIRTY WET TOWEL. HE DIDN'T KNOW WHERE THE FAT MAN WAS LEADING HIM, BUT I FELT SURE IT

Whistle.

Lock.

Penalty.

I looked up in disbelief and saw the Head Editor waving the purple-and-gold penalty flag that signified "Switched Person." A smattering of boos rolled down around me from the stands. My eyes flicked to the board, and it was true, I had slipped out of third person and into first—an amateur's mistake, a kid's blunder. Shame made me duck my head; it was as if, in that moment, I could feel concentrated waves of disgust from the sixty million eyes that watched me.

The ten seconds of the penalty were like a hundred, a thousand. Because all the while The Cranker's machine ratcheted onward, not once slowing or breaking cadence. When my typewriter finally unlocked, I redid the sentence in the proper person and plunged ahead without checking the score. I didn't want to know how far behind I was now. I was afraid that if I did know, it would make me reckless with urgency and push me into another stupid error.

My throat was parched, raw and hot from pipe smoke, and for the first time I thought about the Fuel. It had been a long time since I'd wanted it in the first half of a Face-Off, but I wanted it now. Only I couldn't have it, not until halftime, not without taking a disastrous 20-second Fuel penalty. There had to be less than 600 words left to the end of the quarter, I told myself; I could hold out that long. A top-line pro could do 600 words no matter what the circumstances. A top-line pro, as The Cranker himself had once said, could do 600 words *dead*.

I forced myself to shut out everything from my mind except the prose, the story line. Old page out of the platen, new page in. Old page out, new page in. Speed, speed, but make sure of the grammar, the tense, the phrasing. Still a full 5000 words to go in the match. Still an even chance for a second-half comeback.

THE INTERIOR OF THE WAREHOUSE WAS DANK AND MUSTY AND FILLED WITH CROUCHING SHADOWS LIKE A PLATOON OF EVIL SPIRITS WAITING TO LEAP ON HIM. THEN THERE WAS A FLICKER OF LIGHT AT THE REAR AND IT TOLD SLEDGE THE FAT MAN HAD SWITCHED ON A SMALL POCKET FLASH. GUN IN HAND, HE CREPT STEALTHILY TOWARD THE

My machine locked again.

I jerked my head up, half expecting to see a penalty flag aloft for the third time. But it wasn't a penalty; it was halftime at last. The Line Editor's horn blew. The Cranker's cheering section was chanting *"Culp, Culp, Culp!"*

I had to look at the board then, at the score shining against the sky, and I did: CULP 5000, SACKETT 4796.

Some of the tension drained out of me and I sat there feeling limp, heavy with fatigue. The joints in my fingers were stiff; there was a spot of blood on the tip of my right forefinger where the skin had split near the nail. But the score was all that mattered to me at that moment, and it wasn't as bad as I'd feared. Only 204 words down. I had made up larger margins than that in my career; I could do it again.

Across the Line, Culp was on his feet and staring down at the turf with eyes that gleamed and didn't blink. He wasn't quite so imposing now, strangely. His back was bowed and his hands looked a little shaky—as though he was the one who was trailing by 204 words and facing an uphill battle in the second half.

When I pushed back my own chair and stood up, a sudden sharp pain in my tender hamstring made me clutch at the table edge. I was soaked in sweat and so thirsty I had trouble swallowing. But I didn't reach for the Fuel when my Seconds appeared; in spite of my need I didn't want to take any while I was out here, didn't want to show The Cranker and the crowd and the TriDim audience that I needed it. In the locker room, yes. Just another few minutes.

Two of Culp's Seconds began escorting him off the field toward the tunnel at the south end; he was hanging onto his Fuel container with both hands. I waved away my people and hobbled toward the north tunnel alone.

Fans showered me with roses and confetti as I came into the tunnel. That was a good sign; they hadn't given up on me. The passageway was cool, a welcome relief from the blazing sun, and empty except for the two guards who were stationed there to keep out fans, New-Sport reporters, and anyone else who might try to see me. The Prose Bowl rules were strict: each of the contestants had to spend halftime alone, locked in his respective locker room without typewriter or any other kind of writing tools. Back in '26, the year of the Postal-Rate Riots, a pro named Penny-A-Word Gordon had been disqualified for cheating when officials found out another wordsmith, hired by Gordon's agent, had written a fast 1000-word continuation during the break and delivered it to Gordon, who then revised it with a pen, memorized it, and used it to build up an early third-quarter lead. The incident had caused a pretty large scandal at the time, and the Prose Bowl people weren't about to let it happen again.

As soon as I came into the locker room, the familiar writer's-office odors of sweat, stale tobacco, and spilled Fuel assailed me and made me feel a little better. The Prose Bowl officials were also careful about creating the proper atmosphere; they wanted each of the contestants to feel at home. Behind me the door panel whispered shut and locked itself electronically, but I was already on my way to where the Fuel container sat waiting on the desk.

I measured out three ounces, tossed it off, and waited for it to work its magic. It didn't take long; the last of the tension and most of the lassitude were gone within seconds. I poured out another three ounces, set it aside, and stripped off my sodden uniform.

While I was showering I thought about The Cranker. His performance in the first half had been flawless: no penalties, unflagging speed, front-line prose. Even his detractors wouldn't be able to find fault with it, or even the slightest indication that he was washed up and about to wilt under the pressure.

So if I was going to beat him I had to do it on talent and speed and desire—all on my own. Nothing came easy in this business or in the Prose Bowl; I'd known that all along. You had to work long and hard if you wanted to win. You had to give your all, and try to stay away from the penalties, and hope that you were good enough and strong enough to come out on top.

No, The Cranker wasn't going to beat himself. And I wasn't going to beat myself either.

I stepped out of the shower, toweled dry, bandaged the wound on my right forefinger, put on a clean tunic, and took the rest of my allotted Fuel an ounce at a time. I could feel my confidence building, solidifying again.

The digital clock on one wall said that there were still nine minutes left in the time-out. I paced around, flexing my leg to keep the hamstring from tightening up. It was quiet in there, almost too quiet—and suddenly I found myself thinking how alone I was. I wished Mort was there so we could discuss strategy; I wished the folks and Sally were there so I could tell them how I felt, how self-assured I was.

But even if they were here, I thought then, would it really make a difference? I'd still be alone, wouldn't I? You were always alone in the pros; your parents, your agent, the Editors, the girl you loved, all of them gave you as much help and support as they could—but they weren't pulpeteers and they just didn't know what it was like to go out time after time and face the machine, the blank sheets of paper, the pressure and pain of millions of words and hundreds of Face-Offs. The only ones who did know what it was like were other pros; only your own could truly understand.

Only your own.

The Cranker?

Were we really opponents, enemies? Or were we soul brothers, bound more closely than any blood relatives because we shared the same basic loneliness?

It was an unnerving thought and I pushed it out of my head. I couldn't go out there and face Culp believing we were one and the same. It would be like going up against myself, trying to overcome myself in a contest that no one could ever win . . .

The door panel unlocked finally, just as the three-minute warning horn blew, and I hurried out of the locker room, down the tunnel past the silent guards and back into the stadium. The last of the marching bands and majorettes were just filing off onto the sidelines. The fans were buzzing, and when they saw me emerge and trot out toward the Line, there were cheers and applause, and the Sackett band began playing my old school song again.

Culp wasn't there yet. But as I reached the Line and took my position, I heard the roar from the stands intensify and his rooting section set up a chant: *"Cranker! Cranker!"* Then I saw him coming out of the south tunnel, not running but walking in a loose rapid gait. Halfway out, he seemed to stagger just a little, then regained his stride. When he stopped across from me I saw that his eyes were still bright and fixed, like shiny nailheads in a block of old gray wood. I wondered how much Fuel he'd had during the time-out. Not that it mattered; it wouldn't have been enough to make a difference.

The Head Editor walked out carrying his flags. I lit my pipe and Culp fired a cigarette; we were both ready. The crowd noise subsided as the Head Editor raised his red flag—and then surged again, as the flag fell and the claxon sounded.

The second half was underway.

My mind was clear and sharp as I dropped into my chair. I had checked my prose printout, waiting at the Line, and I had the rest of my unfinished halftime sentence and the rest of the paragraph already worked out; I punched it down, followed it with three fast paragraphs of descriptive narrative. Build into another action-confrontation scene? No. I was only at the halfway point in the story line, and it would throw my pacing off. I laid in a deft one-line twist, for shock value, and cut away into transition.

"That's it, Sackett! That's how to hack it!"

The approving cheers from the Sackett Boosters and from the rest of the fans were like a fresh shot of Fuel: I could feel my thoughts expanding, settling squarely into the groove. Words poured out of me; phrases, sentences, crisp images. The beat of my typewriter was steady, unrelieved, like a peal of thunder rolling across the hot blue sky.

But it wasn't the only thunder in the Prose Bowl, I realized abruptly. The Cranker's machine was making it too—louder, faster, even more intense. For the first time since the quarter had begun I glanced up at the score.

CULP 6132, SACKETT 5898.

1 couldn't believe it. I had been certain that I was cutting into his lead, that I had closed to within at least 175 words; instead Culp had widened the margin by another 30. The thin edge of fear cut at me again, slicing through the confidence and that feeling of controlled power I always had when I was going good. I was throwing everything I had at the Cranker here in the third period, and it wasn't good enough—he was still pulling away.

I bit down so hard on the stem of my briar that I felt it crack between my teeth. Keep bearing down, I told myself grimly. Don't let up for a second.

HE WAS STILL THINKING ABOUT THE CASE, TRYING TO PUT THE PIECES TOGETHER, WHEN THE TELEPHONE RANG. IT WAS VELDA. "I'VE BEEN WORRIED ABOUT YOU, SAM," HER SOFT PURRING VOICE SAID, AND ALL AT ONCE HE FELT

A BURNING NEED TO SEE HER. SHE WAS THE ONLY PERSON HE COULD TALK TO, THE ONE PERSON IN THE WORLD WHO UNDERSTOOD HOW HE FELT.

"Sackett, Sackett!"

But The Cranker's machine kept on soaring; The Cranker's words kept on racing across the board with relentless speed.

WHEN SHE WAS SURE THE CAPTAIN WAS ASLEEP SHE GOT OUT OF THE BUNK AND PADDED OVER TO WHERE HIS UNIFORM LAY. SHE KNEW WHAT SHE HAD TO DO NOW. SHE ACCEPTED THE TRUTH AT LAST, BECAUSE THE WHOLE TIME SHE HAD BEEN COPULATING WITH THE CAPTAIN HER THOUGHTS HAD BEEN BACK ON DENEB, FULL OF THE SIGHT AND THE SMELL OF GREEN.

"Culp, Culp, Culp!"

The lift from the six ounces of Fuel I'd had in the locker room was gone now and the tension was back, binding the muscles in my fingers and shoulders. The sun seemed to be getting hotter, drawing runnels of sweat from my pores, making my head throb. My words were still coming fast, but the images weren't quite as sharp as they'd been minutes ago, the quality level not quite as high. I didn't care. Speed was all that mattered now; I was willing to sacrifice quality for the maintenance of speed.

CULP 6912, SACKETT 6671.

Down by 241 now; The Cranker had only gained seven words in the last 800. But he had gained them, not I—I couldn't seem to narrow his lead, no matter what I did. I lifted my head, still typing furiously, and stared across at him. His teeth were bared; sweat glistened like oil on his gray skin. Yet his fingers were a sunlit blur on the keys, as if they were independent creatures performing a mad dance.

CLENCHING THE CAPTAIN'S LASER WEAPON IN HER HAND, SHE MADE HER WAY AFT TO WHERE THE LIFECRAFT WERE KEPT. SHE KNEW THE COORDINATES FOR DENEB. SHE WOULD ORDER THE LIFECRAFT'S COMPUTER TO TAKE HER THERE—TAKE HER TO THE PROMISE OF THE GREEN.

A feeling of desperation came into me. Time was running out; there were less than 500 words left to go in the quarter, less than 3000 left in the match. You could make up 250 words in the fourth period of a Face-Off, but you couldn't do it unless you had momentum. And I didn't have it, I couldn't seem to get it. It all belonged to The Cranker.

The fans continued to shriek, creating a wild counterpoint to the thunder of our machines. I imagined I could hear Mort's voice telling me to hold on, keep cranking, and Dad's voice hoarse from shouting, and Sally's voice saying "You can do it, darling, you can do it!"

CULP 7245, SACKETT 7002.

Holding. Down 245 now, but holding.

You can do it, you can do it!

SLEDGE'S EYES GLOWED AS HE LOOKED AT VELDA'S MAGNIFICENT BOSOM. VELDA, THE ONLY WOMAN HE'D WANTED SINCE HIS WIFE LEFT HIM THREE YEARS BEFORE BECAUSE SHE COULDN'T STAND HIS JOB AND THE KIND OF PEOPLE HE DEALT WITH. THE PALMS OF HIS HANDS WERE WET, HOT AND WET WITH DESIRE.

The palms of my hands were hot and wet, but I didn't dare take the time to wipe them dry. Only 150 to go in the quarter now.

HE TOOK HER INTO HIS ARMS. THE FEEL OF

HER VOLUPTUOUS BODY WAS EXQUISITE. HE CRUSHED HIS MOUTH AGAINST HERS, HEARD HER MOAN AS HIS HAND CAME UP AND SLID ACROSS THE CURVE OF HER BREAST. "TAKE ME, SAM," SHE BREATHED HUSKILY AGAINST HIS LIPS. "TEAR MY CLOTHES OFF AND GIVE ME YOUR HOT

I tore page twenty-six out of the typewriter, slapped in page twenty-seven.

LOVE. GIVE IT TO ME NOW, SAM!"

SLEDGE WANTED TO DO JUST THAT. BUT SOMETHING HELD HIM BACK. THEN HE HEARD IT—A SOUND OUT IN THE HALLWAY, A FURTIVE SCRABBLING SOUND LIKE A RAT MAKES. YEAH, HE THOUGHT, A HUMAN RAT. HE LET GO OF VELDA, PULLED OUT HIS FORTY-FIVE, AND SPUN AROUND IN A CROUCH.

My machine locked the instant after I touched the period key; the Line Editor's horn sounded.

The third quarter was over.

I sagged in my chair, only half aware of the crowd noise swelling around me, and peered up at the board. The printout and the numerals blazed like sparks of fire in the sunlight.

CULP 7500, SACKETT 7255.

A deepening fatigue seeped through me, dulling my thoughts. Dimly I saw The Cranker leaning forward across his typewriter, head cradled in his arms; his whole body heaved as if he couldn't get enough air into his lungs. What were the New-Sport announcers saying about him on the TriDim telecast? Did they believe he could maintain his grueling pace for another full quarter?

Did they think I still had a chance to win?

Down 245 with only 2500 left . . .

Culp took his Fuel sitting down this time, with his head tilted back and his throat working spasmodically. I did the same; I felt that if I stood up my knees would buckle and I would sprawl out like a clown. The game plan called for no more than three ounces at the third-quarter break—none at all if I could hold off—but neither Mort not I had counted on me being down as far as I was. I took a full six ounces, praying it would shore up my flagging strength, and even then I had to force myself not to make it nine or ten.

Only it didn't do anything for me, as it had at halftime and as it usually did in competition. No lift at all. My mind remained sluggish and the muscles in my arms and wrists wouldn't relax. The only effect it had was to make my head pound and my stomach feel queasy.

With a minute of the time-out left I loaded my pipe, put a match to the tobacco. The smoke tasted foul and made my head throb all the more painfully. I laid the pipe down and did some slow deep-breathing. On his side of the Line Culp was lighting a fresh cigarette off the butt of an old one. He looked shrunken now, at least ten years older than his age of 57—not formidable at all.

You don't awe me anymore, I told him mentally, trying to psych myself up. I can beat you because I'm as good as you are, I'm *better* than you are. Better, old man, you hear me?

He didn't look at me. He hadn't looked at me once during the entire Face-Off.

The Head Editor's red flag went up. I poised my hands at the ready, shaking my head in an effort to clear away some of the fuzziness. The screaming voices of the fans seemed almost hysterical, full of anticipation and a kind of hunger, like animals waiting for the kill.

All right, I thought, this is it.

The red flag dropped and the claxon blared.

ALL RIGHT, SLEDGE THOUGHT, THIS IS IT. HE

And my mind went blank.

My hands started to tremble; body fluid streamed down my cheeks. Think of a sentence, for God's sake! But it was as if my brain had contracted, squeezed up into a tiny clotted mass that blocked off all subconscious connection.

The Cranker's machine was making thunder again.

HE

Nothing.

"Come on, Sackett! Hack it, hack it!"

HE

HE

Block. I was blocked.

Panic surged through me. I hadn't had a block since my first year in the semi-pro Gothic Romance League; I'd never believed it could happen to me in the Bigs. All the symptoms came rushing in on the heels of the panic: feeling of suffocation, pain in my chest, irregular breathing, nausea, strange sounds coming unbidden from my throat that were the beginnings, not the endings of words.

A volley of boos thudded against my eardrums, like rocks of sound stinging, hurting. I could feel myself whimpering; I had the terrible sensation of imminent collapse across my typewriter.

The stuttering roar of Culp's machine ceased for two or three seconds as he pulled out a completed page and inserted new paper, then began again with a vengeance.

A fragment of memory disgorged itself from the clotted mass inside my head: Mort's voice saying to me a long time ago, "To break a block, you begin at the beginning. Subject.

Object. Noun. Verb. Preposition. Participle. Take one word at a time, build a sentence, and pretty soon the rest will come."

Subject.

Noun. Pronoun.

HE

Verb. Verb.

WENT

HE WENT

Preposition.

TO

HE WENT TO

Object.

THE DOOR AND THREW IT OPEN AND THE FAT MAN WAS THERE, CROUCHED AT THE EDGE OF THE STAIRCASE, A GUN HELD IN HIS FAT FIST. SLEDGE FELT THE RAGE EXPLODE INSIDE HIM. HE DODGED OUT INTO THE HALLWAY, RAISING HIS FORTY-FIVE. THE BIG MAN WOULD FEEL SLEDGE'S FIRE IN HIS FAT PRETTY SOON NOW.

"Sackett, Sackett, Sackett!"

It had all come back in a single wrenching flood; the feeling of mind-shrinkage was gone, and along with it the suffocation, the chest pain, the nausea. But the panic was still there. I had broken the momentary block, I was firing again at full speed but how much time had I lost? How many more words had I fallen behind?

I was afraid to look up at the board. And yet I had to know the score, I had to know if I still had any kind of chance. Fearfully I lifted my eyes, blinking away sweat.

CULP 8015, SACKETT 7369.

The panic dulled and gave way to despair. 650 words down, with less than 2000 to go and The Cranker showing no signs of weakening. Hopeless—it was hopeless.

I was going to lose.

Most of the fans were standing, urging Culp on with great booming cries of his name; they sounded even hungrier now. It struck me then that they wanted to see him humiliate me, pour it on and crush me by a thousand words or more. Well, I wasn't going to give them that satisfaction. I wouldn't be disgraced in front of Mort and my girl and family and thirty million TriDim viewers. I wouldn't quit.

In a frenzy I pounded out the last few lines on page thirty, ripped it free and replaced it. Action, action—draw the scene out for at least three more pages. Adjectives, adverbs, similes. Words. Words.

SLEDGE KICKED THE FAT MAN IN THE GROIN AND SENT HIM TUMBLING DOWN THE STAIRS LIKE A BROKEN SCREAMING DOLL, SCREAMING OUT THE WORDS OF HIS PAIN.

Agony in my head, in my leg, in my wounded forefinger. Roaring in my ears that had nothing to do with the crowd.

CULP 8566, SACKETT 7930.

Gain of 20—twenty words! I wanted to laugh, locked the sound in my throat instead, and made myself glance across at Culp. His body was curved into a humpbacked C, fingers hooked into claws, an expression of torment on his wet face: the strain was starting to tell on him too. But up on the board, his prose still poured out in letters as bright as golden blood.

SHE WAS SO TIRED AS SHE TRUDGED ACROSS THE DUSTY SANDS OF DENEB, SO VERY TIRED. BUT SHE HAD TO GO ON, SHE HAD TO FIND THE GREEN. THE BRIGHT GREEN, THE BEAUTIFUL GREEN, IT SEEMED AS IF THERE HAD NEVER BEEN ANYTHING IN HER LIFE EXCEPT THE SEARCH AND THE NEED FOR THE GREEN.

I imagined again the urgent cries from Sally, from Mom and Dad: "Don't give up, Rex! There's still hope, there's still a chance." Then they faded, and everything else seemed to fade too. I was losing all track of time and place; I felt as if I were being closed into a kind of vacuum. I couldn't hear anything, couldn't see anything but the words, always the words appearing like great and meaningless symbols on the paper and in the sky. It was just The Cranker and me now, alone together in the stadium. Winning and losing didn't even matter any more. All that mattered was the two of us and the job we were compelled to do.

Finished page out, new page in.

THE FAT MAN SAT BLEEDING AGAINST THE WALL WHERE SLEDGE'S SLUGS HAD HURLED HIM. HE WAS STILL ALIVE BUT NOT FOR LONG. "ALL RIGHT, SHAMUS," HE CROAKED, "I'M FINISHED, IT'S BIG CASINO FOR ME. BUT YOU'LL NEVER GET THE DIAMOND. I'LL TAKE IT TO HELL WITH ME FIRST."

Carriage return, tab key.

The board:

CULP 8916, SACKETT 8341.

And The Cranker's prose still coming, still running:

THE BEAST LOOMED BEFORE HER IN THE THICKET AND SHE FELT HER HEART SKIP A BEAT. SHE FELT DIZZY, AS IF SHE WOULD FAINT AT ANY SECOND. I CAN'T GO THROUGH WITH THIS, SHE THOUGHT. HOW CAN I GO ON LIKE THIS? I NEED

Culp's machine stopped chattering then, as if he had come to the end of a page. I was barely aware of its silence at first, but when five or six seconds had passed an awareness penetrated that it hadn't started up again. The noise from the stands seemed to have shifted cadence, to have taken on a different tenor; that penetrated too. I brought my head up and squinted across the Line.

The Cranker was sitting sideways in his chair, waving frantically at the sidelines. And as I watched, one of his Seconds came racing out with a container of Fuel. The Head Editor began waving his blue-and-yellow flag.

Fuel penalty. Culp was taking a 20-second Fuel penalty.

It was the first crack in his rigid control—but I didn't react to it one way or the other. The crack was too small and it had come too late: a 20-second penalty at this stage of the game, with the score at 8960 to 8419, wouldn't make any difference in the outcome. It might enable me to cut the final margin to 400 or less, but that was about all.

I didn't watch The Cranker take his Fuel this time; I just lowered my head and kept on punching, summoning the last reserves of my strength.

"Culp, Culp—give us the pulp!"

As soon as the chant went up from his rooters, I knew that the penalty time was about to elapse. I raised my eyes just long enough to check the score and to see The Cranker hunched over his typewriter, little drops of Fuel leaking down over his chin like lost words.

CULP 8960, SACKETT 8536.

His machine began to hammer again. The illusion that I was about to collapse returned, but it wasn't the result of another block; it was just exhaustion and the terrific mental pressure. My speed was holding and the words were still spewing out as I headed into the final confrontation scene. They seemed jumbled to me, incoherent, but there was no lock and no penalty flag.

SLEDGE KNEW THE UGLY TRUTH NOW AND IT WAS LIKE A KNIFE CARVING PIECES FROM THE

FLESH OF HIS PSYCHE. HE KNEW WHO HAD THE MICAWBER DIAMOND AND WHO HAD HELPED THE FAT MAN MURDER HIS PARTNER.

Thirty-five pages complete and thirty-six in the typewriter.

CULP 9333, SACKETT 8946.

Less than 700 words to go. The Prose Bowl was almost over. Just you and me, Cranker, I thought. Let's get it done.

More words rolled out—fifty, a hundred.

And all at once there was a collective gasping sound from the crowd, the kind of sudden stunned reaction you hear in a packed stadium when something unexpected has happened. It got through to me, made me straighten up.

The Head Editor's brown-and-orange penalty flag, the one that meant "Confused Narrative," was up and semaphoring. I realized then that The Cranker's machine had gone silent. My eyes sought the board and read his printout in disbelief.

"I WANT YOU," SHE SAID TO THE CREATURE, "I WANT YOU AS THE SHORES OF NEPTUNE WANT THE RESTLESS PROBING SEAS AS THE SEAS WANT THE DEPTHS GARBAGE GARBAGE

I kept staring at the board, still typing, my subconscious vomiting out the words of my prose. I couldn't seem to grasp what had happened; Culp's words made no sense to me. Some of the fans were booing lustily. Over in G Section, the Sackett Boosters began chanting with renewed excitement.

"Do it, Rex! Grind that text!"

The Cranker was just sitting there behind his machine with a strange, stricken look on his face. His mouth was open, his lips moving; it seemed like he was talking to himself. Babbling to himself?

I finished page thirty-six, pulled it out blindly, and reached for another sheet of paper. Just as I brought it into the platen, Culp's machine unlocked and he hit the keys again.

But not for long.

I CAN'T WRITE THIS SHIT ANY MORE

Lock into silence. Penalty flag.

I understood: The Cranker had broken under the pressure, the crack had become a crevasse and collapsed his professional control. I had known it to happen before, but never in the Prose Bowl. And never to a pulpeteer who was only a few hundred words from victory.

CULP 9449, SACKETT 9228.

The penalty flag came down.

GARBAGE

And the flag came back up, and the boos echoed like mad epithets in the hot afternoon.

Culp's face was contorted with emotion, wet with something more than sweat—something that could only be tears. He was weeping. The Cranker was *weeping*.

A sense of tragedy, of compassion touched me. And then it was gone, erased by another perception of the radiant numerals on the board—CULP 9449, SACKETT 9296—and a sudden jolt of discovery, belated by fatigue. I was only down by 150 words now; if The Cranker didn't recover at the end of this penalty, if he took yet another one, I would be able to pull even.

I could still beat him.

I could still win the Prose Bowl.

"IT WAS YOU ALL ALONG, VELDA," SLEDGE HAMMERED AT HER. "YOU SET MILES UP FOR THE FAT MAN. NOBODY ELSE BESIDES ME AND MICAWBER KNEW HE WOULD BE GUARDING THE

DIAMOND THAT NIGHT, AND MICAWBER'S IN THE CLEAR."

Penalty flag down.

ALL GARBAGE

Penalty flag up.

Virgin paper into my typewriter. Words, sentences, paragraphs. Another half-page completed.

SHIT, The Cranker's printout said. A rage of boos. And screams, cheers, from G Section.

SACKETT 9481, CULP 9449.

I'd caught up, I'd taken the lead . . .

VELDA REACHED INSIDE THE FRONT OF HER DRESS, BETWEEN HER MAGNIFICENT BREASTS. "YOU WANT THE DIAMOND?" SHE SCREAMED AT HIM. "ALL RIGHT, SAM, HERE IT IS!" SHE HURLED THE GLITTERING STONE AT HIM, THEN DOVE SIDEWAYS TO HER PURSE AND YANKED OUT A SMALL PEARL-HANDLED AUTOMATIC. BUT SHE NEVER HAD THE CHANCE TO USE IT. HATING HER, HATING HIMSELF, HATING THIS ROTTEN PAINFUL BUSINESS HE WAS IN, SLEDGE FIRED TWICE FROM THE HIP.

"Sackett, hack it! Sackett, hack it!"

More words. Clean page. More words.

SACKETT 9702, CULP 9449.

The Cranker was on his feet, stumbling away from his machine, stumbling around in circles on the lonely field, his hands clasped to his face, tears leaking through his shaky old fingers.

TEARS LEAKED FROM SLEDGE'S EYES AS HE LOOKED DOWN AT WHAT WAS LEFT OF THE BEAUTIFUL AND TREACHEROUS VELDA LYING ON THE FLOOR. ALL HE WANTED TO DO NOW WAS TO

GET OUT OF THERE, GO HOME TO SALLY, NO, SALLY HAD LEFT HIM A LONG TIME AGO AND THERE WAS NOBODY WAITING AT HOME ANY MORE. HE WAS SO TIRED HE COULDNT THINK STRAIGHT.

Two of Culp's Seconds had come out on the grass and were steadying him, supporting him between them. Leading him away.

New page, old words. A few more words.

SLEDGE SENT THE CAR SLIDING QUICKLY THROUGH THE COLD WET RAIN, ALONG THE MEAN STREETS OF THE JUNGLE THAT WAS THE CITY. IT WAS ALMOST OVER NOW. HE NEEDED A LONG REST AND HE DIDN'T KNOW IF HE COULD GO ON DOING HIS JOB EVEN AFTER HE'D HAD IT, BUT RIGHT NOW HE DIDN'T CARE.

Pandemonium in the stands.

Word count at 9985.

AND SAM SLEDGE, AS LONELY AND EMPTY AS THE NIGHT ITSELF, DROVE FASTER TOWARD HOME.

THE END.

The claxon sounded.

Above the din the amplified voice of the PA announcer began shouting, "Final score: Rex Sackett 10,000, Leon Culp 9449. Rex Sackett is the new Prose Bowl champion!"

Fans were spilling out of the stands; security personnel came rushing out to throw a protective cordon around me. But I didn't move. I just sat and stared up at the board.

I had won.

And I didn't feel anything at all.

The Cranker was waiting for me in my locker room.

I still wasn't feeling anything when my Seconds delivered me to the door, ten minutes after the final horn. I didn't want to see anybody while I had that emptiness. Not the New-Sport reporters and the TriDim announcers who would be waiting at the victory press conference. Not even Sally, or Mom and Dad, or Mort.

I told the Seconds and the two tunnel guards that I wanted to be alone for a few minutes. Then I went into the locker room, and hurried over to the container of Fuel. I had three ounces poured out and in my hand when Culp came out of the back alcove.

"Hello, kid," he said.

I stared at him. His sudden appearance had taken me by surprise and I couldn't think of anything to say.

"I came over under the stands after they took me off," he said. "One of the guards is a friend of mine and he let me in. You mind?"

A little shakily, I took some of the Fuel. It helped me find my voice. "No," I said, "I don't mind, Cranker."

"Leon," he said. "Just plain Leon Culp. I'm not The Cranker any more."

"Sure you are. You're still The Cranker and you're still the best there is, no matter what happened today. A legend . . ."

He laughed—a hoarse, humorless sound. He'd had a lot more Fuel before coming over here, I could see that. Still, he looked better than he had on the field, more composed.

He said, "Legend? There aren't any legends, kid. Just pros, good and bad. And the best of us are remembered only as long as we keep on winning, stay near the top. Nobody gives a damn about the has-beens and the losers."

"The fans could never forget you—"

"The fans? Hell, you heard them out there when the pressure got to me and I lost it in the stretch. Boos, nothing but boos. It's just a game to them. You think they understand what it's like for us inside, the loneliness and the pain? You think they understand it's not a game for us at all? No, kid, the fans know I'm finished. And so does everybody else in the business."

"You're not finished," I said. "You'll come back again next season."

"Don't be naive. My agent's already called it quits, and there's not another ten-percenter who'll touch me. Or a League Editor either. I'm through in the pros, kid."

"But what'll you do?"

"I don't know," he said. "I never saved any of the money; I'm almost as broke now as when I started thirty-five years ago. Maybe I can get a job coaching in one of the Junior Leagues—anything that'll buy bread and Fuel. It doesn't matter much, I guess."

"It matters to me."

"Does it? Well, you're a pro, you understand the way it is. I figured you might."

There seemed to be a thickness in my throat; I swallowed against it. "I understand," I said.

"Then let me give you a little advice. If you're smart, this will be your last competition too. You've got the prize money; invest it right and you can live on it for the rest of your life; you'll never have to write another line. Go out a winner, kid, because if you don't maybe someday you'll go out just like me."

He raised a hand in a kind of awkward salute and shuffled over to the door panel.

"Cranker—wait."

He turned.

"What you typed out there at the end, about the stuff we

do being garbage. Did you really mean it?"

A small bitter smile curved his mouth. "What do you think, kid?" he said and turned again and went out into the tunnel. The panel slid shut behind him and he was gone.

I sat down in front of the Fuel container. But I didn't want any more of it now; I didn't need it. The emptiness was gone. I could feel again, waves of feeling.

I knew now why I had been so hollow when the Face-Off ended; talking to The Cranker had made me admit the truth. It wasn't because of exhaustion, as I'd wanted to believe. It was because everything he'd said about the business I had intuited myself on the field. And it was because of the insight I'd had at halftime—that The Cranker and I were soul brothers and in going up against him I was going up against myself, that beating him would be, and was, a little like beating myself.

But there was something else too, the most important thing of all. Culp was the one who had broken under the pressure, yet it could just as easily have been Rex Sackett. Could still be Rex Sackett in some other match, some other Prose Bowl—typing GARBAGE GARBAGE and then stumbling around on a lonely field, weeping.

Go out a winner, kid, because if you don't maybe someday you'll go out just like me.

I had already made a decision; I didn't even need to think about it. Sally and my parents would be the first ones I'd tell, then Mort, and after that I would make an official announcement at the press conference.

It was all over for The Cranker and all over for me too.

This would be my last Prose Bowl.